true

AN ELIXIR NOVEL

true

HILARY DUFF

with ELISE ALLEN

SIMON AND SCHUSTER

A simon pulse book

First published in Great Britain in 2013 by Simon & Schuster UK Ltd
A CBS COMPANY

Published in the USA in 2013 by Simon Pulse,
an imprint of Simon & Schuster Children's Division, New York.

ISBN: 978-0-85707-155-2
Ebook ISBN: 978-0-85707-998-5

1 3 5 7 9 10 8 6 4 2

Printed and bound by CPI Group (UK) Ltd, Croydon, CR0 4YY

ALSO BY
HILARY DUFF

elixir

devoted

true

one

CLEA

I've never been so terrified in my life.

I run so hard and fast, my breath scours my throat. I don't even know how long I've been running. Agony spikes my legs with every step, but I can't stop. I don't dare.

It's dark, but I don't want to see. I don't want to hear, either, but I can't help it.

Screams. High-pitched screams. A little girl, tortured—her soul ripped apart. It's awful, and it goes on and on and on . . . my God, when will it stop? It has to stop!

Another scream. A man. I know the voice, but I don't want to know it. I don't want to hear it. I can't. I keep running.

A face leaps out of the darkness, blocking my path. Its size is impossible — as tall as I am, white-pale skin stretching over bloodshot white-orb eyes and a mouth open so wide it could swallow me. I scream, but no sound comes out. I back up, but I can't turn away. The blank eyes lock on mine, and bloody tears start streaming down its cheeks.

I step back into nothingness. The last thing I see is the head exploding into scarlet mist.

I fall backward, flail my arms and legs, catch on nothing. The dirt walls of this pit are out of reach, but I can see them, see the twisted faces undulating just under their surface. I see their clawed fingers reaching out to me. Their susurrant voices call to me in a language I can't understand, but the meaning is clear.

These are my dead, and they're hungry for my company.

The voices keen louder as I plummet. I try to plug my ears, close my eyes, but I can't block them out. They fill my senses until a blinding-sharp pain pierces my spine. I raise my head and see it: a massive metal spike impaled through the middle of my body. I hang on it, twisting help-lessly as the dead souls above claw through their dirt coffins and crawl down to claim me as their own. . . .

"NO!" I scream.

"Clea," a voice says. "Clea, it's okay. . . . It's not real. . . . You're safe now. You're okay."

I hear him, but I feel too foggy to understand. The pain in my back is fading, but my face hurts like something's slicing into it. A rush of cold washes over me, and I don't want to open my eyes. I'm more afraid now than I was sur-rounded by the dead, but the reason why floats out of my grasp. All my attention narrows to the strap of pain eating across my forehead, my eye, my nose. . . .

A seat belt. It's a seat belt. I'm in a car. Of course I'm in a car—I can feel it now, the familiar hum and vibration and movement. I must have fallen asleep slumped against the seat belt.

I sit up and wince away from the sting. The pain in my face ebbs, but other aches and flames explode all over my body. I open my eyes . . .

. . . and see Nico, Rayna's boyfriend, staring down at me. It's dark outside, but I can see him in the streaking headlights from cars going in the opposite direction. He's so tall and broad, he looks stuffed into the backseat, like it's a clown car. He's not belted in; he's braced over me, one hand on the back of the passenger seat and one hand on the seat behind my head, his body tenting mine. Twigs and leaves mat his blond hair and dirt smears his face, but his deep brown eyes grip me. They're so filled with worry and —

Brown eyes.

Nico has blue eyes.

I gasp as I remember everything. I see it all — the maelstrom in the woods, bullets and branches everywhere. . . . Nico — the real one — with the dagger in his hand, his moment of hesitation as he held it above Sage's chest . . . I see Ben tackling him, the horror in Ben's face when he saw the dagger embedded in Nico's stomach. Then Sloane, leaping up and grabbing the dagger, plunging it into Sage and killing him, *killing* him, for real and forever.

I stare down at my hands and see the shadowy mess of dried blood from cradling Sage's body. A bubble of agony rises in the pit of my stomach as I remember his face, vacant and empty, his body lifeless in my arms. . . .

"Clea," Nico says. "Look at me. It's okay."

I do look at him, but only at his eyes. His brown eyes.

"Sage?" I ask.

He smiles, and I see double. It's Nico's face, it is, but that's Sage's slow, sideways smile, and Sage's eyes, Sage's *soul*.

The relief is so overwhelming I can't breathe. I try to throw my arms around him, but the seat belt catches and jars me backward.

"Here," he says. He reaches across me to gently play out slack in the belt, leaning forward so, for just a moment, his neck and cheek are by my lips. My heart pounds, and I breathe deep to take in his scent.

But it's not there. I smell something musky, with a chemical sweetness. And when he pulls the seat belt loose enough that I could easily lean into his arms . . . I don't.

"Thanks," I say instead. I don't touch his hand as I gently take the belt back from him and ease it into place over my chest. "I'm good."

He smiles, but his eyes betray him. He looks wounded, which hurts like a punch, until another image bursts into my head: Sage wrapped in the arms of another woman, kissing her and tearing at her clothes.

He severed our soul connection to be with another woman . . . so why is he looking at me like he loves me?

"Clea?"

It's Ben's voice, and it's as tight as his hands gripping the steering wheel.

"Are you okay?" In the rearview mirror, I see his eyes dart to Sage. "Is she okay?"

"I'm fine," I say. It's not exactly the truth, but there aren't words to explain how I actually feel. "What happened? The last thing I remember . . ."

The last thing I remember is Nico's ravaged body healing right in front of me. But how did I get from there to here?

"You passed out," Ben says. "We carried you back to the car. Nico—*Sage* carried you back to the car."

"I *passed out*?"

Sage laughs—a low chuckle that reverberates deliciously in my stomach. "Was I right?"

I'm clearly on the outside of the joke, and I don't like it. "Were you right about what?"

"Ben was worried about you. I told him you'd be fine . . . just furious at yourself."

I don't know if I'm angry at him because I'm offended, or because I'm annoyed that he's right.

"I'm not the passing-out type."

"You're human, Clea," Sage says. "It's okay." He puts his hand on my cheek, and my skin vibrates at his touch. I don't even realize I'm leaning into its pressure until he moves it to slowly brush back my hair. He does it gently, barely grazing my bruises.

His eyes. I thought I'd never see them again, and now they're looking at me with so much love I want to cry.

"'Human' is simplifying it," Ben cuts in. He looks pointedly at Sage between glances out the windshield. "It's not like she's Blanche DuBois with 'the vapors.' You had a vasovagal response," he continues, turning his eyes to mine. "It's one way the body can react to stress. Your heart rate and blood pressure drop, which reduces blood flow to the brain. I have the same thing when I get shots."

"Really?" Sage asks.

Even in the darkness I can see Ben's face go bright red, but his voice stays strident. "I'm just saying, it's not a sign of weakness or anything. It's normal."

"Well, that's good," I say. "I'd hate to think anything about our situation wasn't normal."

Sage laughs out loud. "She's fine."

He stretches back as far as he can in the cramped space and closes his eyes.

I stare as each streetlight thrusts him into a momentary glow. A couple of minutes ago I couldn't bear to move into his arms; now I'm aching to shift next to him and lay my head against his chest.

But what would happen if I did? Whatever I saw in his eyes just now, it doesn't change what he did. He broke the tie between us. Forever. Didn't he?

Another car streaks past, and in its light I see him wince. He looks pale, too, but I can't really tell—even tanned, Nico's skin is so light it's hard to say. Then he takes a long, measured breath through his nose and presses his lips together. The muscle in his jaw flexes as he concentrates.

"Sage?" I ask. "Are you okay?"

He nods his head, but barely.

"He's having some issues," Ben says. "He's been like that most of the ride. He perked up when you started talking, but mostly it's been that. You know, when he wasn't yelling at me to pull over so he could puke his guts out."

"What do you mean? What's wrong with him?"

Through the rearview mirror, Ben gives me the driest look imaginable. "I honestly don't even know how to begin to answer that question."

"Okay, fine. But I mean . . . is this normal?"

"Normal for a guy whose soul got torn out of one body and thrust into another one that I'd just killed two seconds before? Gee, I don't know. It's not something I deal with every day."

There's an edge of hysteria in his voice, and I realize he's struggling to keep it together.

"You didn't kill Nico. You didn't want that to happen. You were just trying to save Sage."

"Well, I certainly did that, right?"

He laughs, but it's manic. I don't like it.

"Ben—"

Sage's groan cuts me off. "Ben! Now!"

"Crap," Ben mutters. He looks over his shoulder and cuts to the side of the road. We crunch onto its graveled edge, and Sage staggers out of the car. Bent double, he hurls himself to the guardrail and crawls over it. I get out in time to see him stumble down a steep weeded embankment and disappear into the darkness.

"Sage!" I shout. I start to climb the guardrail after him, but Ben takes my arm. It hurts more than it should, and I know it must be covered with more bruises.

"He doesn't want you to see. The last few times he didn't bother."

"That's just stupid. I can handle someone getting sick."

I try to tug away, but Ben's grip tightens.

"What's stupid is *both* of you running around down there in the dark."

I yank my phone out of my pocket and turn it on so Ben can see its glow. "Better?"

"No. It's not exactly a floodlight, Clea. Sage is fine. He'll come back when he's ready."

That's when we hear the scream.

"Sage!" I cry, and rip away from Ben to jump over the guardrail and run blindly down the embankment, trampling through prickly brush until I run into the solid wall of Sage's chest. He wraps one arm around me, but it's not a hug—I can feel him leaning on me for balance.

"I'm okay," he says. "I just stepped wrong and fell. I think I landed on something. My arm . . ."

I press a button on my phone to turn it on. It might not be a floodlight, but it's more than enough to see what he's talking about: a thick slab of glass, what looks like the bottom of a beer bottle, embedded across the inside of his left arm, just above the wrist.

"Oh my God . . . We have to go to the hospital."

"We don't. It hurts like hell, but it's fine."

Before I realize what he's about to do, he grabs the glass with his right hand, yanks it free, and throws it to the ground. A wild gush of blood bubbles up and pours out of him.

"What did you do?"

"I pulled out the glass so it can heal," he says, but his voice sounds a little spacey, and he stares at the torrent of blood as if it's a fascinating curiosity, not a danger to his life. I have to snap him out of it.

"Sage. Sage!"

He isn't paying attention. He's transfixed by his own wound. He might be going into shock. I rip off my hoodie and yell up the hill, "Ben! I need you! Call 9-1-1! And bring a towel or something from the car! NOW!"

I place my hoodie against Sage's soaking arm and press down as hard as I can. He looks at me, childlike confusion in his eyes.

"A cut like that . . . that's nothing. It should heal right away. . . ."

A sticky dampness wets my palms. For the

second time tonight, they're soaking in Sage's blood. I can't stop flashing back to before, and what it felt like to hold his lifeless body. Panic pounds in my head, but I can't let it take over. I won't lose him again. I force myself to calm down and speak with gentle authority.

"Don't talk. I need you to lie down. Slowly. I don't want you falling on anything else."

I can't tell if he really understands what's happening, but he nods and lowers himself to the ground.

"Great," I say. "That's great. Now I'm going to raise your arm over your head."

I kneel over his wrist and press my whole body weight against it. My hoodie squishes between my fingers like a sponge.

"They're on their way!" Ben calls as he crunches down the hill. The ambient glow from the cars on the highway barely reaches us down here, but I can see a vague silhouette of him, and it looks like he's carrying something. Good.

"What happened?" he asks.

"Did you find a towel?"

"I had one in my gym bag. It might not smell too great—I've been pushing pretty hard on the free weights, and I'm up to six miles on the treadmi—"

"Seriously?" I pull the ratty hand towel away from him and press it onto Sage's wound.

"Sorry, I . . . Here, let me do that."

"I've got it."

"Stop. I'm stronger. He needs more pressure. On the count of three: one, two, three."

I pull away, and Ben takes my place. Now that I'm off triage, my mind spins terrible fantasies about all the hideous, flesh-eating bacteria that could live on that sweaty gym towel and get into Sage's bloodstream. My stomach lurches.

I need to focus. I crawl to Sage's face and smooth the hair off his forehead. His skin is clammy and cool to the touch. I bend down close so he can see me. He has a half smile on his face, like he still can't comprehend what's happening.

"I feel so . . . strange," he says.

"Yeah," I say, keeping my voice light. "That's what happens when you almost bleed to death."

He shakes his head. "I can't bleed to death."

"They drained the Elixir from you. You won't heal anymore. Not like you used to."

"But . . . my stomach. I saw it heal. *You* saw it heal."

"That wasn't the Elixir," Ben says, his voice strained from the pressure he's putting on Sage's wrist. "It was the soul transfer. I don't know how exactly it works, but it heals the host body."

Healed, maybe. Now Sage's breath comes in fast, shallow gasps, and I know it's only a matter of minutes before he loses consciousness. I run my hand over his cheek and will him to stay awake and alive.

"You're going to be fine," I say. "You just need to take better care of yourself from now on, okay?"

Sage gives a single puffing laugh. "I guess you're not the only one who's human."

We hear the ambulance siren, and Ben says, "Go up to the road so they see us. I'll stay here and keep the pressure on."

I hate to leave Sage's side, but I lean down and kiss his cheek, then race up the embankment. I stand in the glow of our car headlights, jump up and down, wave my arms, and scream.

It works. The paramedics pull over, and two EMTs make quick work of stabilizing Sage enough to put him on a stretcher and bring him back to the ambulance. Ben and I don't have to say anything to each other; we know I'll ride in the ambulance and he'll follow in the car.

Sage spends the drive unconscious, hooked to a machine that measures his heart rate and blood pressure. I sit on a hard, cold bench that keeps me close enough to hold his hand. One of the EMTs is with us, but he doesn't ask any questions. I guess for him it's not so strange to find three people covered in dirt and twigs, battered, bruised, and bleeding out on the side of the road.

He's so fragile. I never thought of Sage that way, but it's true. There's so much I don't understand, but I do know our time is precious. I can't waste any more of it with doubts. "You'll be okay," I whisper into his ear. "I'm here for you. No matter what."

I keep my promise and stay close as Sage is transferred from the ambulance to the emergency room. They wheel him into a room with two beds, but the other one's blocked by a curtain. Sage is still out, so I tell the nurses what happened . . . more or less. They listen, then make me step into the hall while they pull another curtain around him and go to work.

It's only after I plop down in the most uncomfortable molded plastic chair that I realize I have no idea where we are. We started in Vermont, I know that, but I'm not sure how long I was out. Are we closer to home? I scan the hall for clues, but there's nothing except doctors and nurses moving briskly between doorways, and a lot of anonymous equipment.

My phone vibrates. It's Ben. He's in the waiting room. They won't let him in, so he says he'll wait until I can come out.

"And don't forget," he says, "Sage is Nico."

"Right, because that was totally going to slip my mind."

"I mean officially. For paperwork and stuff. He has Nico's wallet in his pocket, with all Nico's ID."

I hadn't even thought about that, but it's the kind of detail Ben would never let slip.

"Thanks," I say. "Sorry."

"No problem. I'm here. Text or call if you need anything."

I hang up quickly as I see a man in a white lab coat stroll into Sage's room, and I duck in after him. He disappears behind the curtain around Sage's bed and I hover by the door, staring at the red container of USED SHARPS for the eternity until he emerges again.

"How is he?"

Something flashes in the doctor's eyes when he looks my way, and I know he recognizes me. I'm far from famous, but my family's filled with some of the decade's biggest political players, not least of whom is my mom, Senator Victoria Weston. We're not the Kennedys or the Clintons, but I've had my picture in enough newspapers and magazines that some people know who I am. The doctor's professional enough that he doesn't say anything. He also doesn't question if I'm authorized to hear private information about Sage, so maybe the recognition is good.

"He needed stitches and blood," the doctor says, "but he'll be fine. The biggest worry in a case like this is infection, so we have him on IV antibiotics plus a painkiller, and we'll want to give him a tetanus shot . . . unless he's had one in the last ten years?"

"I'm not sure," I say.

"That's fine. We'll do it as a precaution. We'll want him here for another couple hours, then you can take him home. The stitches will dissolve on their own, so just keep his wound clean and dry, and bring him right back to the emergency room if he develops a fever or shows any sign of infection."

"I will."

"Good." He nods toward the curtain around Sage's bed. "You can go in, if you'd like. He'll drift in and out of sleep, but when I left him, he was awake."

I don't even respond; I dart past him and pull aside the curtain.

Sage is awake, but he looks like he's in a daze. He stares down at the back of his good hand, where the IV line disappears into his skin. His other hand is bandaged, to hide the brand-new stitches. For a moment, I concentrate hard enough to stencil Sage's old body over this one: dark hair; angular face with the slightest growth of stubble around the mouth, chin, and neck; sinewy body; Italian olive skin and chocolate eyes.

It's an impossible image to hold. The eyes are still there, but every other part of him is milk-fed farm boy.

"Thank you for bringing me here," he says. His voice is relaxed and dreamy.

"Of course. You were hurt."

"No . . . I mean thank you for letting me see this." He raises his hand with the tube snaking out of it, then turns to indicate the IV stand and electric monitor that beeps as it measures his vitals. "Magnificent."

"Magnificent?"

It sounds bizarre, until I think about it. "I guess

if you haven't been in a hospital for five hundred years, it's pretty amazing."

"Five hundred years? I knew it was a long time . . . but that long?"

"What do you mean? Don't you remember?"

He shakes his head. "I remember Magda, that old woman in Japan . . . the things she showed us . . . images from a long time ago. People . . . you and Ben, but you didn't look like yourselves. And I was there too, but I always looked the same, year after year after year. . . ."

His dreamy voice rings out in the room, and I dart my eyes to the curtain separating us from the next bed. I lean in close to Sage and whisper, "That's because you never died. You drank the Elixir of Life, remember?"

"I do remember. . . . I remember knowing about the Elixir, and that I've had a long life . . . but I don't remember *living* it. Does that make sense?"

"No. Not really."

"That day I met you in Brazil . . . I took one look at you, and knew I loved you, at that moment and forever."

"Right. Because you already knew me."

"I suppose . . ."

"You suppose?"

He squeezes his brows together, as if struggling to find something in his mind. Then he gives up and shrugs. "It's not there. I don't remember. I remember *you*. Clea Raymond. The minute you and I met . . . *that's* when my memories start."

two

CLEA

A moment later Sage is fast asleep. He drifts off smiling, still holding my hand in his. The bandages make his unconscious grip feel inhuman, and I slide away from his touch.

Or maybe it's not the bandages that leave me cold. *The minute you and I met . . .* that's *when my memories start.* They're the kind of words that would make Rayna swoon, but that was never Sage's and my story. That started long before I was even alive. It brought us together, a soul connection that stretched throughout history.

A soul connection.

Could that be what happened? When he cut our soul connection, did he keep our love, but lose our past? Or is his memory loss from the soul transfer?

There's so much I don't understand, and I feel like I have to before he and I can figure out what's next. Or explain things to Rayna. I shudder. I definitely need to know more before I talk to her. How can I expect her to handle all this if I can't comprehend it myself?

I don't want to wake Sage, so I pull a chair next to the bed and text Ben. I ask him to scope out the closest motel, then I check my phone's GPS to see where we are. Vermont. We haven't left Vermont, so we hadn't been driving very long when I woke up in the car. I feel a little better knowing that even if I passed out, it was only for a bit.

Sage twitches and thrashes as he sleeps, murmuring angry words I try to understand but can't. It hurts to hear him—whatever torture he feels, it rips at me, too. When he curls into a ball and whimpers like a kitten, I can't take it anymore.

"Shhh, shhh, it's okay." I reach for him, but the minute my hand touches his damp forehead, he bolts upright and grabs me. He clutches my wrist in both his hands. His grip is so hard it hurts, but I remind myself that this is the man I love; I shouldn't be afraid.

"Help me," he rasps. His eyes are wide open, but he's looking through and past me. I don't even know if he's really awake. He's trembling, and I put my other hand over his and rub them gently, trying to calm him down.

"I want to help you, Sage. Tell me what you need."

Instead he closes his eyes and falls back onto the bed, still now and sleeping soundly. At some point I nap too—a dreamless sleep that ends when I feel someone right in front of me and open my eyes to see Nico's—*Sage's*—grinning face. He puts a finger to his lips.

"We're busting out of here."

"What?" I feel woozy, and there's a crick in my neck.

"Aw, dude, come on!" calls a voice from the door. "I'm supposed to wheel you out! It's my job! I'm gonna get in trouble!"

Standing in the doorway is a mountain of an orderly, who can't be more than nineteen. He holds the handles of an empty wheelchair and shifts uncertainly from side to side, darting his eyes around for whatever authority might come yell at him if he doesn't get Sage into the chair. I don't know why he's worried; he takes up the entire doorway. There's no way out except through him. Sage sighs and reluctantly plops into the chair. In his new body, he and the orderly look like they're teammates on a college football team: an injured quarterback getting pushed to the locker room by his oversize linebacker.

"I used your phone and called Ben," Sage says as he's wheeled through the halls. "Hope you don't mind."

When the doors outside slide open, Ben's already there, smiling ironically as he leans against his car.

"Your chariot," he offers.

I'm squinting against the low morning sun, so it takes a second to see what he means. The "chariot" looks more like a junkyard swamp creature. Ben is the most cautious driver in the world; he washes his car every two weeks and is meticulous about regular service appointments. He's been driving his little black Corolla since he bought it himself—used—when he was eighteen. Now it's coated in a thick layer of dirt, pitted with dents and scratches, and the entire undercarriage is matted with clots of mud and grass.

"Oh, Ben . . ."

"You should see the driver's side," he says, then shakes his head. "Actually, you shouldn't. Trust me."

"I'm sorry."

Ben shrugs. "Badge of honor, right? Besides, you're always telling me it's time to get something new." He opens the back door, and the Offensive Tackle Orderly puts the brakes on Sage's wheelchair and comes around front to lift him out with a bear hug, but Sage stops him with a perfectly arched eyebrow.

"Uh-uh," he says. "I'm fine."

He climbs into Ben's car and I follow, tossing the orderly a "thank you" on the way.

"So where to now?" Sage asks once Ben's inside and driving.

"I already have orders from Clea," Ben responds. "The nearest motel's just ten minutes away."

"Motel?" Sage asks.

"You should rest," I say, though it sounds disingenuous. Whatever haunted his dreams before, Sage seems fine now. Almost back to himself.

Maybe I'm just making excuses to put off facing Rayna.

Maybe . . . but I *am* tired, and Ben must be exhausted. As for Sage, he's trying not to show it, but I can tell his playful burst of energy is fading. His head lolls against the back of his seat, and he struggles to keep his eyes open. It's not surprising; he's on hard-core antibiotics — the kind of thing he's never experienced before. At least, his soul hasn't. Maybe his body has?

Whatever — we all need to rest.

Ben pulls off the highway into a patch of barren blacktop, nestled onto which is a Denny's, a Chevron, and the generic box of a Red Roof Inn. It's perfect. He pulls up to the office and turns around in his seat. Sage's eyes have closed, and Ben keeps his voice low. "I'll go in if you want to stay with him."

"Great, thanks."

But Ben doesn't leave the car. He furrows his brow and sucks air through his teeth.

"What?" I ask.

"It's just . . . I'm thinking . . . one room, right? Two beds and we bring in a cot?"

"You want to chaperone?"

"No," Ben says, blushing. "I just . . . we've all

been through a lot . . . especially, you know . . . and . . ."

"Two rooms," Sage says without moving or opening his eyes. "Adjoining. Ben bunks with me."

"I'm on it," Ben says, and slips out of the car before I can object. When he's gone, I unbuckle my seat belt and move closer to Sage.

"Open your eyes," I whisper.

He does, and everything else blurs as I focus in on only those brown orbs. "It's true. The eyes really are the windows to the soul. That's why yours stayed the same."

"Did they?"

"You haven't looked at yourself in the mirror," I realize.

"I've caught glances, that's all."

Unbelievable. To me the change in Sage is so glaring and obvious, it didn't even occur to me that he hadn't fully seen it.

"When we get to the room," I say, "you'll get a good look."

"Like it or not."

That's when it hits me. He's afraid. I've seen Sage face death without fear. It didn't even occur to me that he'd be afraid to see his own reflection.

I slip my hand into his. It's clammy, but this time it's not from the gash in his wrist.

"If it helps, I know exactly how you feel. I've seen myself in another body."

Something shifts in Sage's eyes, and I feel like he's looking for more.

"I know how strange it is," I tell him, "when you see yourself, but it isn't you. I remember the first time I dreamed of us, before I'd even seen you outside my pictures. I was Delia, singing at a club where you played piano. You watched me when I performed. . . ."

I can see it in my head, and it takes my breath away. At the time I thought it was the most vivid dream I'd ever had: me as a singer in the 1920s, tied to a mob boss named Eddie but sneaking off to meet Sage, the secret love of my life. It was wild and romantic and dangerous . . . and completely real, though I didn't know that right away. It was a memory of a past life Sage and I had shared. Yet when I look at him now . . . he isn't sharing it at all. There's nothing in his eyes except wistful sadness.

"You don't remember any of that, do you?"

Sage shakes his head. "I remember seeing it— bits of it—through Magda. But it's not like I lived it. I *did*, I understand I did. But it doesn't feel that way. I've lost the memories."

"Just for now," I assure him, though there's no way I can know. "Maybe they'll come back to you in dreams. The way they did for me."

"I hope so. I don't want to lose any time with you, Clea. Not even time in the past. It's just . . ."

His eyes are filled with the same look I remember from my dreams. The one that promises he's mine, now and forever. But there's something else in there too. There's pain and . . . doubt?

"What is it?"

"I might know why I can't remember. I made a choice, while we were apart. I saw you and . . ." His eyes drift to the driver's seat. "I don't even know if it was real, but I . . ."

He clenches his jaw, and my stomach hurts because I know what he's seeing. In a fit of jealousy over Sage and another woman, I'd tried to seduce Ben. Even though Sage was miles away, he saw it — the incriminating part, before Ben rejected me. *That's* why he broke our soul connection.

"Sage . . . look at me . . . please."

He doesn't want to, but he does. The mix of anger, hurt, and guilt I see there is almost unbearable, but I won't let myself look away. I take his hand and squeeze it. "I know what you did," I say, "and I know why. And if that's the reason you can't remember . . . if that past is gone for us . . . that's okay."

"How can it be okay? Clea, while we were apart . . ."

I know he's about to tell me about Lila, but I can't hear him say it out loud. The only saving grace of Sage's new body is that it's not the one I see tangled together with Lila's every time I blink.

"I already know," I say. "Just like you know what I did. What I *tried* to do. It didn't . . . I wasn't . . . I was jealous. What you saw . . . that's all that happened."

It's my penance that I have to watch this sink in. Sage slips his hand out of mine and stares at me like he's seeing me for the first time. He did what he did with Lila because he was held captive. Playing along with her was his only way to maybe get back to me, and he only gave in completely when he thought I didn't want him anymore. What I did with Ben had been on purpose, designed to wound. A million questions fight in Sage's eyes, and he leans back into his seat with a heavy sigh.

"So the past is gone forever," he says. "All we have is now."

"Isn't that all anyone has?"

Before Sage can answer, the door opens and Ben flops into the driver's seat. He leans back and hands two key cards each to Sage and me before starting up the car. If he notices the tension in the air, or Sage's glare, he doesn't show it.

"I shall now drive you both to our very own parking spot," he says. "It's quite luxe."

Silence.

"What?" Ben asks. "What'd I miss?"

"Nothing," Sage says. "We're speechless over the luxe accommodations. Let's check them out."

Ben cocks his head, clearly debating whether to ask any more questions, but he decides against it, and we drive all of ten feet before we park. As we get out of the car, Ben heads to the trunk and grabs three plastic Walgreens bags, all filled to bursting.

"What are those?" I ask.

"It's not just the accommodations that are luxe. While you were in the ER, I got us all brand-new outfits. Very chichi."

The minute he says it, I realize how harsh and heavy my dirty and bloodstained jeans and T-shirt feel against my skin. I don't care what kind of clothes Ben managed to find at a drugstore in the middle of the night; they sound like heaven.

"Two rooms, two showers," I say. "I call first round."

"Wrestle you for the other one?" Ben asks Sage as we climb the stairs to the second floor. "I've been working out. I might be able to take you."

Sage gives Ben a half smile, but it doesn't reach his eyes, and his fists are balled at his thighs. "You go first. You don't want to wrestle me."

"Two-ten and two-eleven," Ben says. He gestures for me to open one of the doors while he gets the other.

Sage follows behind me like a shadow as we walk into room 211. It's a simple box, decorated in browns and creams, and the light streaming in the open curtains at the far end gives us a perfect view of what we're waiting to see.

The mirror.

It's on the door of the closet, just a few feet in. We approach it wordlessly, and I take Sage's hand as he turns to face it head-on.

He stares, but his eyes are unreadable. He lets go of me and touches his own face, watching his fingers as they trace its new contours.

He reaches up to finger a thatch of blond hair, so much shorter than the dark mane he wore all his life. He clenches his fists; sinews stand out in his forearms. He gazes down at his thick biceps, watching them grow as he flexes.

It's weird, but watching him discover Nico's body, I'm blown away by how completely *Sage* he is. Nico was always languid and relaxed; the man who stares into the mirror is tightly coiled. He leans forward slightly, ready to spring into action, his jaw tensed and gaze steeled.

I can't know what Sage sees when he looks at his new self, but I see the final proof that the man I love is alive and well.

He moves closer to his reflection. "Nico didn't have brown eyes?"

"Blue. Strikingly blue. I remember them. Rayna said they reminded her of a place we went on the Italian Riviera, where the water's so clear you can see down to forever." I smile, remembering how Rayna sighed over the cliché like she was the first one who ever said anything like it. Then my throat clenches. "I don't know how I'm going to tell her."

Sage puts an arm around me. I know he's trying to comfort me, but I see our reflection through

Rayna's eyes: Nico, the man she thought was the love of her life, cuddling with me, her best friend. Even if she realizes the eyes are a different color, even if she sees that the way he stands, the way he acts, the way he does *everything* is different from what she knew, she'll still see Nico. I know because I'd do the same thing if it were me. I'd want to see the man I love so badly that I *would* see him, even if he wasn't really there.

Am I doing that? Am I seeing Sage inside Nico's body because I want to?

No. That's crazy. Every word that comes out of Sage's mouth proves that it's him. And even though it'll be hard for her, eventually Rayna will understand that, too.

I hope.

There's a knock on the door connecting our two rooms, and I open it for Ben.

"Clothing delivery," he says, holding out one of the plastic bags. "I thought you'd want it before you got in the shower. Yours are on the bed in there," he adds to Sage. Then he frowns. "Clea? Is everything okay?"

"Rayna," I reply.

Ben's whole body deflates. "I know. Are you going to call her?"

"I can't do it over the phone. When I see her."

Ben nods. He opens his mouth like he's going to say something comforting, like maybe that it'll all be okay, but I think he knows better. He offers a halfhearted smile, then walks back into the other room. I turn back to Sage, who's still gazing at his reflection.

"You don't have to wait for Ben to finish," I offer. "You can use the shower in here."

"That's okay, you go ahead."

I watch him stare at his own face for another moment and try to imagine what he's feeling. It was bizarre enough for me to see visions of Olivia, Catherine, Anneline, and Delia and know my soul was inside them, but if I actually looked in the mirror right now and saw one of them staring back at me . . . I'm not sure how I'd handle it.

I grab my bag of clothes, lock myself in the tiny bathroom, and turn the shower as hot as it can go. The whole room is steamy before I strip down, pull open the shower door, and test the water with my palm. It's just this side of scalding. Perfect. I step under the powerful stream and shiver as it pelts my skin. I wash my hair three times, using the entire bottle of motel shampoo, and take huge satisfaction in the swirls of filthy water that flow down the drain. When I've soaped and washed every bit of the last twenty-four hours of grime off me, I lean my back against the wall and slide down until I'm sitting in the stall, my ears filled only with the patter of water, steam filling my lungs. I'd stay like this all day, but too soon the water loses its biting heat, and I turn it off before it gets too cold.

I dry off and pull out Ben's purchases: a purple pullover sweatshirt two sizes too big for me, and a green pair of sweatpants with elastic just below the knee. The material's thin but soft and cozy; to me they feel like the finest silk. I throw my wet towel over the clothes I took off and kick the pile into a corner. I don't ever want to see them again.

When I come out of the bathroom, the room smells like coffee, and Ben's sitting on the king-size bed sipping a mug of it as he laughs at a rerun of *The Daily Show*. His sweatshirt is orange, even bigger on him than mine is on me, and he wears it with a pair of red sweatpants.

"I should have you shop for all my clothes," I say as I head toward the door to the other room. "You're a genius with color. I can't wait to see how you dressed Sage."

"He's asleep," Ben says, and when I ease open

the door, I see he's right. This room has two double beds, and Sage is sprawled out on one of them, completely unconscious. His sweats match and fit him perfectly, though they're an eye-popping shade of electric blue. I ease the door closed again and stack the pillows so I can lean my back against them when I sit on the bed next to Ben.

He takes a sip of his coffee and winces. "For once I'm jealous that you don't need this stuff. The coffeemaker in here is awful."

At another time, small talk over bad coffee and Jon Stewart would be fun, but not right now. "Tell me about the soul transfer," I say. "Why do you think Sage was so sick?"

"I don't know. Maybe it's because Nico's stomach was cut open. Or maybe it's just something that can happen, like the bends."

"But does it mean anything? Is Sage okay?"

"Clea, I don't know. I'm not an expert on soul transfers."

"You knew it healed Nico's body."

"I checked out some things in your dad's books, after we came back from Japan." My father and Ben had been close, and shared a love of all things paranormal. Ben was the one person who knew about most of my dad's research in that area, the only one who knew his way around it all. "There wasn't a lot, and I didn't go looking for more."

Because you hoped it wouldn't happen, I think but don't say. *You hoped Sage would just stay away.*

I really need to stop. From getting involved with a serious girlfriend, to pushing me away when I threw myself at him, to saving Sage's life, Ben has proven that he's not pining for me or fighting with Sage to win me over. He didn't go looking for more information on soul transfers back then because Sage was gone and it wasn't relevant. I need to give him more credit. He may have come between Sage and me in the past, both in this life and lives before, but maybe what Sage said goes for Ben, too: The past is gone forever. All we have is now.

"I can go through his studio when we get back," Ben says. "Look around and see if there's anything I missed."

"Thanks. That'd be great."

He yawns and runs his hands over his face. He looks rumpled, and I realize he hasn't slept since before we left for Vermont yesterday.

"My God, Ben, you need to sleep. You look like the walking dead."

Ben nods to the other room. "Actually, I think

even the walking dead looks better than me right now."

We both wince. "Not funny," Ben admits. "Maybe I should sleep. You should too."

He staggers into the other room, and I watch the rest of *The Daily Show* before I turn off the TV and curl under the covers. Even with the curtains drawn, the midmorning sun glows inside, but it doesn't stop me from drifting off.

I wake to a dead man standing over me and have to stifle a scream before I remember it's Sage.

"Can I stay here? I just want to be close to you," he says, his voice soft and low.

I nod and pull back the covers so he can crawl in beside me. He spoons against my back, and I stiffen against the unfamiliar shape, the too-thick arms with their too-tight squeeze. But the longer I'm curled inside his grasp, the more sheltered I feel. I dreamily imagine that this was how it was always meant to be, that Sage's soul needed a new home to be truly human, and this home will protect us both for the rest of our lives. I cuddle in closer to him, and my final thought before I drift off is that I hope this time our happiness can last.

true

I wake to darkness and the smell of coffee. I'm alone in bed, and without Sage I feel tiny on a huge island of covers. I hear muffled voices from the next room, so I slip to the floor, pad across, and push open the adjoining door.

Ben and Sage sit back on the double beds, their faces and colorful sweats bathed in the light from the TV they stare at intently.

"Breadfruit . . .? Broadfist . . .?" Sage murmurs.

"Brownfish!" Ben whisper-shouts. "Brownfish in Bay!"

"What's 'Brownfish in Bay'?"

"I'd like to solve the puzzle, Pat," comes a voice from the TV. "It's 'Breakfast in Bed.'"

"That's correct!" lilts Pat Sajak, and a blast of music confirms the triumph.

"'Breakfast in Bed'?" Ben gapes.

"Like that's less common than 'Brownfish in Bay'?" Sage asks.

"'Brownfish in Bay' was a perfectly reasonable guess."

"Oh my God, you're an old married couple," I say, and both guys' faces share a look of surprise as they wheel to face me.

"It's true," Ben sighs playfully. "He doesn't even stay in our bedroom anymore. Imagine my surprise when I woke up in the middle of the night all alone."

Sage isn't even listening to him. The minute he realized I was there, he jumped out of bed, and now he envelops me in a hug that feels as safe as a cocoon. "How do you feel?" he whispers into my hair.

"Wonderful. How about you?"

"Never better."

I consider dragging him back into bed so we can wake up lazily together, like a normal couple living a normal life.

"Good enough to travel?" Ben asks. "We should probably hit the road."

He's right. There will be plenty of time for normalcy, but not before we've cleared one last hurdle: going home and talking to Rayna.

"After we eat," Sage says. "I'm ravenous."

We quickly check out and walk across the street to Denny's. It's April—springtime—but there's still a winter chill in the air as the sun slips below the horizon. I huddle close to Sage and he wraps his arm around me until we're inside. We each gobble a quick Grand Slam breakfast—*two* Grand Slam breakfasts, in Sage's case, since he vacuums up his own plus half of mine and Ben's.

The minute he finishes, he practically falls asleep in the booth, then asks if I'll sit up front on the ride to my house so he can sprawl out in the back.

Seconds after we hit the road, Sage is out. I can hear his rhythmic breathing in the seat behind me. It's soothing, and I zone out as I listen and stare out the windshield at the now-starlit sky.

Ben clears his throat.

"So," he says softly, peering at Sage in the rear-view mirror, "everything was . . . okay with the two of you last night?"

"Ben . . ."

"I'm not asking for any ulterior reason. Which I shouldn't have to say, and maybe I don't have to say, but I feel like I should say."

When I don't respond right away, he adds, "Your line now should be, 'You don't say.'"

"Hmm, that would have been clever."

"I thought so."

We pass under a streetlight, and I turn to see its light wash over Sage. He sleeps contorted around his seat belt. He didn't want to wear it, since he'd be more comfortable without, but I'd held up his bandaged wrist and reminded him he had to take care of himself if we were going to have a long life together.

"Everything was okay," I tell Ben. "He's fine."

"Good." He's silent for a while, then adds, "He kind of reminds me of a lion."

"A lion?"

"Lions sleep for about twenty hours a day, and spend the rest of their time hunting and eating." He nods toward the backseat and adds, "It's like the man can't get rested or full."

"It's also like a baby, isn't it? Maybe getting a new body is like being reborn."

"Maybe. I hope so. A baby's pretty harmless. A lion not so much."

My hackles rise, and I feel my body tense. "What are you trying to say?"

"Nothing. Honestly, nothing. If this is happily ever after for you guys, I'm thrilled. I mean it. All I'm saying, as your friend, is be careful. Maybe take it slow."

"Thanks, Dad." I can't help the sarcastic bite in my voice, but Ben takes it in stride.

"Exactly. If he were here to say it, he would."

That stops me, because it's true . . . which still doesn't mean I want to admit it out loud. I let a little time pass, then turn up the radio to drown out the silence.

It's midnight by the time we pull onto my property. My eyes strain for the guesthouse as we move along the driveway. Maybe it'll be dark. Maybe I'll get a reprieve until morning.

No such luck. The light's on in Rayna's room. Worse, I can see her moving toward the window. She knows we're back. I have to talk to her now.

"Pull around the side. I'll head to Rayna's while you wake up Sage and take him to the guest room. I don't want her to see him until I explain."

"I'll meet you over there. I want to talk to her too. If it wasn't for me—"

"Ben, please . . . I really want her to hear everything from me."

He thinks about it, then nods. He pulls the car around the far side of the house, and I slip out the minute he stops. Knowing Rayna, she's already out the door and on her way. I don't have a lot of time if I'm going to keep her from Sage.

"Thanks, Ben."

"Good luck."

I'll need it.

three

RAYNA

Downward Dog . . . lower into Plank . . . Chaturanga . . . rise into Cobra . . . push into Upward-Facing Dog . . .

I have two sticks of sandalwood incense burning on my dresser, and Clea's housekeeper, Piri, came through today for her twice-monthly stint in our house, so the carpet gives off lingering whiffs of vanilla Carpet Fresh . . . but mostly what I smell is horse manure.

This is what happens when you spend practically an entire day doing yoga in a stable.

It's not that I'm Miss Horsewoman, though I pretend to be, and my mom loves it. It's her job to take care of Senator Victoria Weston's horses—has been since forever. This works well, since Senator Weston and my mom are best friends, I'm best friends with the senator's daughter, Clea, and Mom working on the estate means we get to live in a guesthouse on the property. It's also a bonus that my mom loves horses; she'd do the job for free.

I do not love horses. I don't dislike them or anything. They're beautiful, and it's almost impossible not to look good on a horse, which is a major plus. But taking care of horses involves a lot of time around dust, mud, and of course, horse poop.

Horse poop is not my thing. Or it wasn't . . . until Nico.

Thinking his name makes my heart race, and I feel like I'm going to jump out of my skin.

Deep breath . . . extend the right leg to the sky . . . swing it through to Runner's Pose . . .

Better.

Horse poop didn't bother Nico.

Doesn't. Doesn't bother Nico.

Senator Weston hired Nico to help my mom, and I knew the second we met that we were destined to be together. The boy wears Wranglers—

seriously, *Wranglers*—and makes them look hot. He grew up on a ranch in Montana, says the word "golly" without irony, and has a body that makes Ryan Gosling look like pre-diet Jonah Hill.

In other words, he's almost unbearably adorable. And since he's a horse person, of course I had to become a horse person if I wanted to snag him. While he's gone, I feel closer to him if I'm around the stables—and by extension the smell of horse manure. I stayed out there until it got too dark and, frankly, smelly for me to take it, but it's like the scent has lodged itself permanently into my nose. Even after a shower with perfumed soap and shampoo, I can still smell it, just not as strongly.

That's okay. It reminds me of Nico, so it'll help me hold it together until he comes back.

If he comes back.

Pins and needles ripple on my skin. *Stop. Stop thinking that way.* I move into Reverse Warrior, digging deeper and breathing into the backbend until everything except my breath and my muscles fades away.

I wonder if there's a world record for continuous hours of yoga. Maybe I should go for it. As it is, whenever I stop I end up biting at my fingernails, and that's no good because Nico likes when

I scratch his shoulder blades. He calls them his "angel bones," which is something only he could get away with and not sound like a complete dork. But if my nails are all ragged, they'll hurt his back and I'll feel bad and . . .

I tumble out of Half Moon Pose and feel something lodge in my heel.

"Ow!"

I sit on the floor and examine the damage. Despite the vanilla scent, I'm thinking Piri didn't actually vacuum that well, because I just stepped on an open staple. Why there was an open staple in my rug is anyone's guess, but my bigger concern is that it's stuck in my heel and it hurts. I yank it out, and twin bulbs of blood bloom in its place, the teeth marks from an elfin vampire.

Ugh.

I hop to the bathroom, grab Band-Aids and Neosporin, then hop back into my room, where I flip on the television so MTV's pregnant teens can keep me company while I doctor myself up. I figure they can also distract me from the horrible feeling in the pit of my stomach that something is very wrong with Nico. It's more than a feeling; it's a psychic knowledge, deep in my soul.

If I were Clea, I'd tell myself I'm just being

overemotional. But that's not how things work in the paranormal world. In the paranormal world, psychic knowledge means something. You'd think Clea would know this, since she's been swimming in paranormal since she found Sage in the background of our European vacation pictures. That's the thing with Clea, though, and I say this with love: She is in complete denial of anything that isn't logical. It took her ages to believe that Sage is her soulmate. And even when she did believe it, when she admitted her dreams were visions of past lives, she couldn't let go and enjoy this incredible gift of true love. She had to dissect it, and worry about which version of her Sage loved best, or what he did for satisfaction during the decades—*decades*—in which her soul hadn't yet returned to Earth.

I, on the other hand, know from paranormal. I've had a Ouija board correctly tell me the initials of my first boyfriend, I've watched every episode of *Ghost Hunters*, and I was among the first to fall in love with *Twilight*. I'm much more prepared than Clea to be involved in a paranormal romance.

Not that I wanted that. I mean, I used to. I looked at Clea and Sage's epic love affair and thought it would be so thrilling to have something like that, but the truth is, I was perfectly happy to settle down with someone whose picture could be in the dictionary next to the word "normal."

Then Nico confessed that his family's in some kind of cult tied to the Elixir that's kept Sage alive for hundreds of years, and all those born into the cult are cursed to die before they're thirty.

Sounds crazy, right? But I heard his stories. Nico's dad died when he was twenty-eight, his sister was killed in a freak car accident when she was sixteen, and his little brother died at *three* because he was born with an insanely rare disorder. Crazy cursed cult is the *least* bizarre explanation. Plus, I'm pretty sure Nico's head would explode if he tried to lie.

So there we go; I had a boyfriend doomed to die young. We had no choice but to squeeze a lifetime of happiness into a few short years, constantly looking over our shoulders at the ticking clock of doom. . . .

Okay, yes, it was horrible . . . but it was also pretty romantic. Like, *Titanic* romantic. At least it was when Nico first told me. He was so earnest about it. He said he'd dedicated his life to breaking the curse. Not for himself—he didn't care as much about himself—he wanted to break it for his remaining younger siblings, and for the other kids born into the cult who otherwise would never have a chance.

"My own life never mattered much to me," he'd said. "Not until I met you. I want to spend the rest of my life with you, Rayna. And maybe it's selfish, but I want that life to be a lot longer than the next nine years. I want to marry you. I want to have kids with you. *Lots* of kids."

Whoa.

I've never wanted to have kids, but the way Nico looked at me when he said that made me see it. We'd get a farm somewhere, we'd save up for "date nights," I'd stay home with our five little kids while Nico worked . . . maybe I'd even homeschool the kids. If I was going to do that, I'd probably have to pay more attention in school. I wondered if Helmut Lang would ever start making aprons.

I was so far off in happy homemaker land I didn't even realize he was down on one knee until he took my hand and squeezed it. Then I screamed.

"YES! Oh my God, YES! Nico . . ."

"Wait. Rayna, I can't ask you to marry me right now. That wouldn't be fair."

"But you're down on one knee."

"Because I'm proposing to propose. I'd give you a promise ring if I had one."

"A promise ring? That's . . . adorable."

"I mean it. I already wrote to my mom. She has my grandmother's wedding ring, and I told her to get it polished up and ready, because one day soon it's gonna be yours."

I threw my arms around him and kissed him. "Maybe we shouldn't wait," I said.

"You don't understand—"

"I do. I believe the curse is real. I just don't care. You said you want to be with me for the rest of your life. I want that too, and I want it no matter how long it is."

Nico smiled, but he shook his head. "I love you, Rayna. I love you too much to let you marry me the way things are now. Let me break the curse . . . and I *will* break the curse . . . and then we'll do it up right. All I'm asking now is to know you want the same thing I want. Tell me that, and I'll have the strength to do anything."

"Anything?" I gave him my best wicked smile, but of course he didn't get it.

"Yeah, anything. Why, what did you . . . oh."

I had just peeled off my shirt and thrown it on the floor. Even he couldn't misread that one. His lips curled into a smile and he pulled me to him, and it was like in an end-of-the-world disaster movie, where the main characters know this could be their last time together, and they throw themselves into each other with complete abandon and it's all heady and dramatic and wonderful. . . .

But I didn't *really* think it was the end of the world. That didn't happen until afterward, when Nico took off with Clea and Ben to find Sage. He was excited about it; he was sure when they found him, he'd break the curse once and for all. I wanted to go too, but he wouldn't let me. He said it was too dangerous.

Dangerous wasn't supposed to be part of the deal. I mean, it was all fine and good to *feel* like we were cheating death each second we were together, but I didn't want him to actually risk his life.

"Don't go," I whispered.

"I have to," he said. "But I'll come back. I promise."

I believed it . . . but that was a little over twenty-four hours ago. I wish I could say I still believe it, but . . .

Okay, the *16 and Pregnant* girl is in labor, and it looks nightmarish. If Nico does come back — *when* he comes back? — maybe he'll be okay with one kid instead of "lots." And maybe we can wait twenty years or so before we have it. Or maybe we'll just dress up little dogs.

I turn off the TV and hear something outside. The gate at the end of the driveway, rolling open. My heart thumps against my chest. I'm dying to race to the window, but I'm afraid to look. My parents are both asleep, Senator Weston and her entourage are out of town, Piri and the rest of the household staff are long gone for the day. It has to be them . . . but is Nico there too?

If I don't look, if I pretend I don't know they're back, then I won't have to hear the bad news. I can spend all night believing he's okay.

Unless he *is* okay. Then putting it off just makes it longer until we're back together.

I race to the window and press myself against it just in time to see headlights and what looks like the outline of Ben's car cruise past my house, past the main parking area for Clea's house, and around the corner to the back.

Oh shit. Oh hell. I can't breathe. I hear myself hyperventilating, and everything's getting swimmy.

Ben wouldn't drive around to the back like that if Nico was okay. He wouldn't. He and Clea have to know I'm freaking out. If everything was okay, they'd park right in front of my door and run inside. The house is on a gated estate; it's not like we keep the door locked. The only way he'd avoid my house is if he's avoiding me, and the only reason he'd avoid me is if he and Clea didn't want to give me bad news.

As I fly down the stairs and out the door, I come up with other reasons Ben could have driven around back. If they succeeded and saved Sage, Clea and Sage might want to slip inside and have some privacy. Or *Clea* could be the one hurt, so they're pulling up to a door that's closer to her room. That's got to be it. And I'm not a horrible friend for thinking it, because if she was *really* hurt, she'd be in the hospital, not at home. She's just sort of hurt. Sort of hurt's no big deal, but it would be weird for Nico to excuse himself and come see me when she's even sort of hurt and they're getting her all situated and comfortable, so it's good I'm coming to him.

That's why I'm running so fast. It's not that I'm worried about Nico. Nico's fine. I'm running to help Clea.

I race barefoot across my front lawn and the mulched grove that separates my house from Clea's, then onto the smooth blacktop of the long, winding driveway. Little stabs of pain pierce my sore heel with every step, and I can just picture myself limping the last few feet to Nico. I see it so clearly, I don't even notice something's in front of me until I slam into it and topple to the ground.

"Rayna?"

It's Clea, but that doesn't make sense. She's supposed to be hurt, and Nico and Ben and maybe Sage are supposed to be helping her up to her room.

"Are you okay?" she asks. She holds out her hand so I can grab it and pull myself off the ground, but when I look up at her and see her face, I freeze.

"No," I say. "No, no, no, no, no."

I won't look at her. Then she won't say it. I

squeeze my eyes shut and shake my head and wait for her to go away.

She doesn't. She thumps down next to me.

"I'm so sorry, Rayna. Nico . . ."

"Don't say it. Don't say it."

"I'm sorry. Rayna . . ."

Clea puts a hand on my knee and ducks low, trying to catch my eye. I look up at her . . . and my stomach rolls over.

She looks happy.

Not like jumping-up-and-down happy, but I know her. Before she left last night she was shattered. Now she looks sad and sympathetic, but she's not. Not really.

"Sage," I say. "You found him. He's okay."

The words taste like acid in my mouth. Clea's eyes get wide, and her mouth curves into a shocked little O, but she doesn't deny it.

"He's okay, but Nico isn't." It's an accusation, and Clea knows it. Now she's the one who won't look at me.

"Sage is . . . He's okay. Yes."

"And Nico's not." The words are awful, but I feel stronger for saying them, like they're arrows I'm shooting into Clea's body. I know they're hurting her; I can see her body hunching over around the wound. It feels good. I want to do even more.

Of course Sage is okay. Of course. He belongs to Clea, who always gets what she wants. It's been like that forever. She's the celebrity. She's the one everyone wants to photograph and interview and hover around. She's the star of the movie, the one who always gets the happy ending. I'm the side-kick; no one cares if my heart gets broken.

Clea shakes her head. Nico's not okay. "I'm so sorry, Rayna."

She wraps her arms around me, and I freak out. "Get *off* me!" I shove her away, but I can still feel her on me, and it's so gross I can't even deal. I hold out my hands in front of me, my body rigid and my fingers bared like claws.

"Rayna . . . what are you doing?"

She comes toward me *again*!

"Stop! Get *away* from me!" I scramble to my feet. She's so small down on the ground, her per-fect blond hair and big blue eyes and fake-angel face. I want to kick her right in her chin.

"I know how you feel—"

"You know how I *feel*?" I snarl. "How? It all worked out for you, Clea, just the way you wanted it!"

"No!" she says, her lying eyes wide now, like

that'll make me believe her. "I never wanted any-thing to happen to Nico."

"You did if it would save Sage. He's the impor-tant one, right? You and Sage and your 'eternal' love. Nico and I, we didn't have anything like that. He was just a guy and I'll get over him, so it doesn't matter what happens to him. That's what you think!"

"No!"

"It's *exactly* what you think!"

"That's not true."

"Then why did you let him go with you and Ben?"

Clea's mouth is open to answer, but nothing comes out. Of course not. There's nothing she can say.

"You can't answer that, can you?"

She does, but she looks at the ground when she says it, not at me. "He *wanted* to come."

"So? You could have stopped him. You could have left without him. You could have left him here with *me*."

Clea buries her face in her hands. When she looks up, her eyes are puffy, all ready to cry fake tears. "It's okay if you're mad at me," she says. "I understand."

"I don't give a shit if you understand! I don't need your permission! My God . . ." I tangle my fingers in my hair and pull. I'm so angry I can't handle it. I don't know *how* to handle it, so I want to rip and tear and destroy, but all I can do is lean into Clea's face and scream as loud as I can.

"Rayna!"

The voice is panicked. It's my mom, lumbering toward us in her robe, her tight curls sleep-matted to one side of her head.

"I heard screaming. . . ." Mom looks around, her eyes darting back and forth between Clea and me. "What's going on?"

I can't answer.

Nico's gone.

He's gone.

I don't feel myself start to cry. One minute I'm standing there and the next I'm on my knees, bent double, sobbing and choking.

Mom's arms wrap around me and I hear the worry in her voice. "Rayna? Baby, what happened? Clea?"

I don't want to hear how Clea explains everything to my mom. I pull out of the bear hug and stagger to my feet. I lock eyes with Clea for what I hope is the last time ever.

"This is all your fault," I say. "*You* did it, and I will never, *never* forgive you."

Clea and Mom both say things as I walk away, but the tears are coming harder than ever now. I can't hear them, and I don't want to see them. I wave them off and run back home, run back to my room and fling myself onto my bed. I pull all my pillows close and curl into a ball around them, squeezing them tight while I cry and cry and cry.

I'll probably cry forever.

four

CLEA

"She's right," I tell Ben. "It's my fault Nico's dead. I sacrificed him to save Sage."

Ben and I are in the family room. We face each other on the couch, our feet pulled up and our backs against the armrests. He'd found me outside, sitting in the grass after I'd tried to explain to Wanda. I hadn't made a lot of sense, but once she'd understood that Nico was gone, she hadn't listened for more. She'd left without another word. She probably believed what Rayna said, that it was my fault.

Within the last seventy-two hours I've been shot at, threatened at knifepoint, and pummeled head to toe by flying rocks and branches, but nothing scared me like Rayna's face when she said I killed Nico. Nothing hurt as badly, either. I think I'd still be sitting out there, wounded in the grass, if it weren't for Ben. He gathered me under his arm and led me inside to my favorite of the over-stuffed gray couches, then draped an afghan over me while he went into the kitchen and made tea. Azteca Fire, mixed with sugar and almond milk, my favorite comfort drink. I clutched the mug in both hands, and only after I'd taken several sips did he ask what happened.

"It's not your fault Nico's dead," Ben says now. "It's mine."

"No, it's not. You can't blame yourself."

"Pretty sure I can, seeing as I actively tackled him into a knife."

"You actively tackled him *away* from killing another man. What happened after that . . . just happened. He fell. It's my fault he was even there to begin with."

"How do you figure that?"

"I should have made him stay home with Rayna!" I insist.

"The man's a house," Ben says. "You really think you could have stopped him?"

"Why not? You think *you* could have stopped gravity!"

He leans forward to make another point, and I'm set to volley it back . . . when he slumps back into the cushions. "Wow . . . Can we stop fighting about which one of us is more horrible?"

I find a weak smile. "Okay. Is Sage upstairs?"

Ben nods. "Asleep. I didn't know where you'd want him, so I put him in the guest room."

"Great. Thanks."

Neither one of us says anything for a long time. It feels good, though. I'm so down-to-my-bones exhausted, I can't imagine trying to chat . . . but with Ben I don't have to. There's no pressure. Even after everything, I can just sit with him in silence and feel totally at home.

Then I wonder. "Did you ever tell Suzanne about . . ."

I wave my hand in the air. It's the only way I can think to sum up everything Ben might have told his girlfriend—all about Ben's past lives, and mine, and how time after time the men with Ben's soul caused tragedy for me and Sage.

Ben gives a short laugh and shakes his head.

I smile too. I know Suzanne—she works for my mom—and there is no way I can see her handling that kind of conversation.

"Just as well," he says. "She ended it. You know, after . . ."

Now it's his turn to drift off, but I know what he means. After the night on the beach, when I threw myself at him. Maybe it should make me uncomfortable that he brings it up, but it doesn't. I can tell he's not upset about it—not anymore. He just says it that way because he's as tired as I am; it would take too much energy to do anything else.

"You okay?"

"Oh yeah. It's better, actually. Suzanne's a little bit . . . high-maintenance."

I nod sympathetically, but a second later we both burst out laughing because Suzanne isn't just a little high-maintenance, she's *ridiculously* high-maintenance. But even that isn't it. Not really. We laugh because it feels so good and light and easy and *normal*, and we both keep going until we're gasping for air. When I'm completely spent I take a deep breath and let it out in a long sigh . . . at the exact same time Ben does, which starts us laughing all over again.

"Can I tell you something?" Ben says once we

settle down. I expect him to make some kind of joke and I narrow my eyes at him. "I really admire you."

I scan his face for sarcasm, but there's none. "Me?" I ask. "For what?

"I admire your strength. Most people, if they faced even a fraction of the stuff you've had to deal with, they'd land in a psych ward. But you handle it."

"Badly."

"Better than you think."

Ben has a throw pillow in his lap and twines his fingers in and out of its fringe. The circles under his eyes . . . I've seen him pull three all-nighters in a row juggling work and research projects, but I've never seen him look this tired. More than tired. He looks worn, like . . .

Like an old soul.

Ben can talk all he wants about how much I've had to handle, but he's dealt with just as much. Nico's death was the worst. If I were any kind of friend at all, I'd urge him to go on vacation someplace far away, where he could try and forget everything that happened this year. The Elixir is gone; my drama doesn't have drag him down anymore.

The problem is there's no one else I can ask.

"I'm hoping you can do me a favor," I say.

"You want me to do some research and find out what's going on with Sage."

It's exactly what I want, but now I can't say it. I can't drag him into this any deeper.

"No," I say. "Forget I mentioned it. You've done enough."

"Stop. Of course I'll help you. We're friends."

He looks at me meaningfully, and I hear what he *doesn't* say: that all the confusion about our relationship is in the past. We're friends. That's all, and that's everything."

"Thank you," I say.

"Happy to do it. I figure I'll start with the library at Yale. They have an ancient text collection that's pretty extensive. The content is all over the place, but you can find some incredible things if you know where to look."

"And you know where to look?"

"I do."

He starts to say something else, but cuts himself off with a yawn that lasts forever. "I think maybe I'd better take off," he says instead. "I'll call you tomorrow."

"Good night. Thanks again."

I watch until he leaves, then I go up to the spare room, where Sage lies tangled in the covers. There's a pen and small steno notebook on the night table, a Post-it stuck on the cover. I pick it up and see Ben's scrawl.

Pls write down anything unusual.

Of course. He knew I'd ask for his help, and he knew he'd come through for me. *Anything unusual*, though . . . I could fill the entire notebook. Maybe I should. Maybe if I write everything out, I could give it to Rayna and explain.

I messed up so badly with her. As I wash up and get changed, I run through the whole awful conversation. I should have handled it differently . . . but how? What was I going to do, just let her see Sage without explaining? Wouldn't it be worse if she thought she had Nico back, actually saw him in front of her, and *then* found out the truth?

I don't know. I can't tell her in writing, though. That wouldn't be fair. I have to talk to her, face-to-face. Just not now. It's one in the morning. I'll wait until tomorrow.

Even asleep, Sage looks like himself. Rayna once told me Nico sprawls when he sleeps, every limb splayed out in all directions. Not Sage. He's coiled, tensed, ready to leap into action. His soul calls out to me, and I'm dying to crawl into bed next to him, but I keep seeing him through Rayna's eyes. I feel so guilty, like I deserve to be punished. I sentence myself to a night alone and pad back to my room for a long night of dreams in which I have the same horrible conversation with Rayna, again and again.

The second I wake up, I call her. "Hey," I tell her voice mail. "I know you hate me right now, and that's okay. I just . . . I really need to talk to you. Rayna, please call me. I need to explain some things to you. Please. I love you."

This is so hard. I have no idea how to make this okay, but every minute she doesn't know the whole truth makes me feel like I'm lying to her. I text and e-mail her.

"AAAAAIIIIIEEEEEE!!!!!!"

I jump up and race downstairs, hoping desperately that our housekeeper, Piri, saw a mouse, or a spider, or someone crossing the threshold without touching the jamb to discharge evil spirits . . . anything except Sage. The last thing in the universe I need is for Piri to tell Rayna she saw her boyfriend. It would be a complete dis —

Crap.

Piri stands in the entranceway to the kitchen, frozen. Her shopping bags dangle from the ends of her fingertips as she stares in mute horror at Sage, who hums to himself as he pulls a skillet out of the oven. He's wearing Piri's ASK ME ABOUT MY SAUSAGE apron, which Dad found in Hungary and thought was so funny he bought it for her, despite the fact that it made no sense on a woman.

The minute Piri sees me and knows she has an audience, she drops her shopping bags. They stay upright, which is nowhere near dramatic enough for her, so she taps one with her foot until it topples and spills apples, squash, and zucchini across the room. Sage has to have seen it happen, but he ignores it.

"I made breakfast!" he crows, and tilts the skillet so I can see inside. "Shrimp and asparagus frittata with parmesan!"

Piri points a bony finger at him, and her mouth curls in disgust. "You!"

My heart pounds. With old-world superstitious certainty, Piri always knew there was something different about Sage. Can she tell it's really him inside Nico's body?

She stalks to him and peers into the skillet with

such disdain I'm sure she's going to spit in it. "You went through my kitchen. You used my parmesan."

I almost cry, I'm so relieved. Let her hate Sage for violating her cheese. I'm cool with that.

"I did," Sage says. "And if you'd like to join us, I think you'll be very pleased with the results."

Piri's eyes squint, and I know I have to get Sage out of the room as soon as possible. Even if she doesn't suspect anything yet, she will soon. The real Nico would be falling all over himself to apologize, bowing and scraping until he won back Piri's approval. Sage . . . not so much.

"Smells good, right?" he says.

Note to self: When a man takes over someone else's body, probably best to brief that man on what the previous resident was like.

Then again, Sage trying to play Nico would probably be an even worse disaster.

"Why are you here," Piri asks, "without your girlfriend?"

His eyes shoot toward me. No. Bad.

"*Because*," I say brightly, "*Nico* wants to make *Rayna* a special meal, and he's practicing to make sure he gets it right."

Piri sniffs the air, a human lie detector. She glares up at Sage, her hands on her hips. "No more cooking in my kitchen. You want eggs? I'll make you eggs."

She reaches for the pan, but Sage sweeps it out of the way. "I'm good, thanks. These are fine."

Piri's face turns beet red as Sage flips the frittata onto a plate, then sweeps into the dining room, which I can see he's already set with our plates and a huge pot of tea. "You coming, Clea?"

"In a sec."

I bend close to Piri. "Sorry about Nico. He's not himself. I think he and Rayna are going through a little rough patch."

"Hmmm."

"He really wants to make it up to her with a surprise. So when you see her, please don't say anything about this. You probably shouldn't say anything to Wanda, either. She's not so great at keeping secrets."

"Hmmm."

Piri's mouth is a thin straight line, and she won't stop glaring into the dining room at Sage. The best thing I can do is get him out of her sight.

"Breakfast looks great," I say as I walk into the dining room. Behind me, I hear Piri mutter in Hungarian and make spitting noises. I lower my voice. "Maybe we should take it upstairs."

"Why? I have the table all laid out."

"Just . . . trust me. Please." I already have our plates and utensils in my hands and am on my way out of the room. Sage follows with the teapot. "It's only until I talk to Rayna," I add when we're out of earshot. "I don't want Piri saying anything to her, so the less she sees of you the better."

Sage follows me into my room and I lock the door behind us, then spread a blanket on the floor. I arrange our plates on it. "Like a picnic. It's good, right?"

"It's perfect," Sage says.

But he's not looking at breakfast, he's looking at me. He moves closer, shrinking the distance between us, and my heart thuds in my chest. I've been in a scattered frenzy all morning, but now the whole world shrinks down to only me and Sage. When he reaches out and cups my cheek in his hand, I close my eyes to savor his touch.

"This is life now," he says, his voice a caress. "You and me. No one chasing us, no one stopping us . . . nothing in our way."

He leans in, and I lose myself in his kiss. I wrap my arms around his neck and pull him closer, breathing him in, this new scent I already love. There's nothing else in the universe except this moment, his lips, his body, his touch. When he pulls away, I keep my eyes closed, waiting for more.

It doesn't come.

I open my eyes and see Sage sitting on the blanket eating his half of the frittata, a mischievous gleam in his eye. "Delicious. You should try it."

With a rueful smile, I sit across from him and pour myself a cup of tea. Like last night, Sage races through his own food, then ogles mine like a cheetah stalking a gazelle.

"You can have it," I offer. "It's great; I'm just not hungry."

"You sure?"

I barely nod before he grabs the plate and wolfs down every bite, then looks around the room like he's on the prowl for more.

"Do you feel okay?" I ask.

"I feel great. Just hungry, that's all."

I shouldn't worry. He's hungry, that's not a big deal. This body just needs more fuel than the one he's used to.

I think that, but I don't believe it. Something feels off—something beyond the obvious—but maybe that's because I'm still reeling from everything that's happened.

"Think I can go downstairs and raid the pantry without your housekeeper having a fit?" he asks.

Immediately I think about Rayna—the whole reason I can't let Piri see more of Sage—and I check my phone to see if she's returned my texts or e-mails. She hasn't.

"I can grab you something," I say. "Then I should go. I really need to try to talk to Rayna."

Sage reaches out to squeeze my hand. "Forget the food," he says. "Go see her. And don't worry. All you have to do is tell her the truth."

I nod, hoping he's right, then make him promise to lock the door after I leave. I wait in the hall until I hear the click, then slip downstairs and make my way to Rayna's house. Wanda answers the door, but she stands like a bouncer, arms folded, her wide body blocking any way inside. "Rayna isn't ready to see you," she says. "Maybe you shouldn't come back over until you hear differently."

Wanda's my second mom. This is the first time she's ever seen me without pulling me into a bear hug. Her cold stare makes me feel like I'm three years old and I've been bad. My voice is small when I say, "I understand," and trudge the miles that now stretch between her house and mine.

I knock gently on the door to my room when I

get back, but Sage doesn't answer. He's probably asleep. And I'm locked out. There are definite flaws to my Keep Sage Away From Piri plan. I consider sifting through Dad's books in the study, but I know it would take me all day to do what Ben could manage in a half hour. It would feel incredible to go for a long run . . . but all my running clothes are, of course, locked inside my room.

Then inspiration hits. My favorite cameras are locked away, but I have others all over the house. I grab one from the living room, sling it over my shoulder, and run outside. I consider driving to the beach, but I want to be close when Sage gets up, so I go back upstairs and spend the next hour snapping unique angles of the furniture, keepsakes, and subtle imperfections I usually take for granted. I shoot like I'm ravenous for the project, without a single worry about whether a shot will be perfect. I work on pure instinct. It's absolutely magical, and time slips away. When I'm done, I run to my mom's room and upload them to her computer. She doesn't have the right software to do anything serious with them, but I can at least click through and check them out.

Every picture leaves me cold.

I can't understand why. They're exactly what I'd hoped for—fresh angles on images I always knew—but each one makes my heart sink. I enlarge each bigger and bigger, scanning for the flaw I can't pinpoint.

Until it hits me.

Of course I'm disappointed. Sage isn't in any of them.

I hadn't even realized I was searching for him. I knew he wouldn't be there—he hasn't appeared in my pictures since he cut our soul connection. Still, I expected to find him, a treasure tucked into the background of my favorite shots.

I get it now. That's why I was so excited to take pictures in the first place. I thought I'd have the chance to see him again. Not in Nico's body, but in the one I've known in my soul all my life. Sage is alive and with me . . . but I'll also never see him again.

"NO! OUT! OUT!"

Crap! How did I not hear my door open? For the second time today I race downstairs to find Piri and Sage in the kitchen. This time Piri's wielding a spatula at Sage, who stands next to the refrigerator with his hands raised in mock surrender. In one of them he holds a hunk of parmesan cheese, in the other a bag of asparagus stalks.

"Easy," he says. "I'm just making breakfast."

"No!" she shouts. "Out of the kitchen!"

"Nico?" I ask, but he doesn't respond until I put a hand on his shoulder and squeeze. "*Nico? What are you doing?*"

"I'm *trying* to make us breakfast."

"This is not right," Piri grumbles. "This is very bad."

"Leave it alone!" Sage snaps. "Clea, can you get her out of the kitchen, please?"

I flash Piri a quick smile, then turn back to Sage. "Actually, maybe we should go back upstairs."

"No. I'm hungry. I'm making breakfast."

I sidle close to him and speak through clenched teeth. "You already made breakfast. I said if you were hungry I'd get you something else." I shoot a meaningful glance toward Piri, but there's no comprehension in his eyes.

"What are you talking about?"

"Breakfast. The frittata you made."

"How do you know I'm making a frittata?"

A chill runs down my spine. "Can you come upstairs with me?" I ask Sage.

"I'm cooking."

"Please?"

He grimaces, but he puts down the parmesan and asparagus and follows me out of the room. As we pass the dining room, I notice the table is again set for a meal, complete with another big pot of tea.

"You do know you already made breakfast this morning, right?" I ask when we're halfway up the stairs.

"What do you mean?"

"You got up, you set the dining room table, and you made a frittata. Piri walked in and yelled at you for being in her kitchen, then we went up to my room to eat. We had a picnic on the floor. You don't remember that?"

"I don't know what you're talking about."

We reach my door and I pull it open. Sure enough, the floor is still littered with the detritus of our meal. Sage stares.

"What's all this?"

"I told you."

"No . . . this wasn't here before."

"It was. You just don't remember."

He looks worried, so I reach out and put a hand on his arm. He yanks away.

"It *wasn't*!"

"It's okay," I say, masking my fear with a calm

voice. "You forgot. I'm sure it doesn't mean anything . . ."

"I didn't forget! I'm telling you, Clea, *these were
not here!*"

His face twists in anger. I suddenly feel very
small next to his huge, muscular frame, and my
voice sounds meek and scared.

"Please don't yell at me."

"Then stop lying to me!" He stomps on one of the
plates, shattering it.

"What's happening up there?" Piri calls. She's
coming upstairs. I can tell. I know something is
very wrong with Sage—there's no way he'd talk
to me like this otherwise—but right now I have to
deal with Piri, and I can't do it unless Sage stays
calm and out of my way. I have to placate him.
Hating myself a little, I hang my head.

"I'm so sorry. . . . It was my mistake. I don't
know what I was thinking. Forget everything I
said. I'll go get something to clean this up and I'll
be right back, okay?" I reach out and squeeze his
hand while I give him a hopeful smile, and after a
moment he grudgingly returns the squeeze.

I slip out the door, close it behind me, race for
the stairs . . . and practically slam into Piri. She
carries a broom like a club over one shoulder.

"We call 9-1-1," she says when she sees me. "Now."

"No. We do *not* call 9-1-1."

"I don't like that boy, Clea. He changed."

"You're wrong," I lie. "Nico's upset about Rayna. That's it. He's fine, I'm fine . . . everything is fine. It's better than fine. For you, I mean."

I'm scrambling, and Piri can tell. She narrows her eyes and looks at me dubiously. "For me?"

"Yes! I want to show you something. Come with me." From my bedroom I hear the crunch of Sage stepping on another plate, but I ignore it and lead Piri downstairs. I have no idea what I'm going to show her until I hit the first floor and inspiration strikes.

"Piri, my mom and I have been talking, and we want to send you on a vacation."

I rattle off what I hope is a convincing story about Mom and I wanting to surprise her with a trip to Foxwoods Casino, a place I know she loves. I say we want to send her immediately— this very night—but I'm going to book it right now with her in the room so she can choose any spa treatments or shows she wants to see.

We've never done anything like this for her before, and I can tell she thinks it's strange. Yet once I pick up the phone and start making arrangements she gets excited and jumps in with a huge list of requests. It's cute, actually—her eyes light up and she bounces up and down excitedly as I book everything she asks for. She even squeals when I get her a table close to the stage for a magic show she's dying to catch. It makes me wish Mom and I *had* planned this for her ages ago.

By the time I'm off the phone, Piri isn't concerned about anything except her trip. She gives me a huge bear hug and kisses me on both cheeks before practically floating out of the house. I hold my breath as I watch her car on the security camera screens, terrified she'll see Wanda or Rayna and stop to chat and say something about Nico, but thankfully it doesn't happen.

"Did I do this?"

I jump at the voice. It's Sage, and he holds one of the broken plates like he doesn't know how it got into his hand.

"Yes."

"I don't remember it."

He looks crushed. Whatever made him so violent before is gone now, and he's so sad I just want to make him feel better. "Don't worry," I say. "You're disoriented, that's all."

"Sure." He still stares at the plate. Gently I pull it from him and set it on the table, then take his hands in mine. I wait for him to look at me, and when he does, when I see the man I love in those eyes, I can't help but be positive everything will turn out okay.

"Listen to me," I say. "You're going to be fine."

"You can't know that."

"I do, though. Whatever else is happening . . . you're here. You're human. We're together. We have our whole lives ahead of us, and we're starting them right now."

For the rest of the day, I don't leave Sage's side. He never gets angry, and he doesn't have any more memory lapses. When he takes a nap, I write down what happened in the steno book Ben left me, then watch Sage sleep. I want to be the first thing he sees when he wakes up. I want to ground him in reality.

It works. He wakes up with a smile and pulls me onto the bed next to him.

The rest of the day is perfect. We're constantly touching. We watch movies and TV shows and play board games and talk constantly about nothing deeper or more serious than what's right in front of us. I love it. Everything feels so simple and light and *right*. Weirdly enough, it's the most normal day of our entire relationship.

Still, something nags at me all day. I don't want to say anything and risk killing the mood, but by dinnertime I can't help it.

"Okay," I say once the delivery guy leaves and we're on the couch chowing on pizza, "I have to ask you something."

"Yeah?"

"You really don't remember anything about our past? About Olivia, Catherine, or any of the others?"

He shakes his head.

"But . . . you still . . ." I can't bring myself to say the word I want to say. Not as a question. ". . . care about me?"

I feel so weak and vulnerable as I look into his eyes, but the warmth there is endless. He holds out his hand, and I rest mine inside it.

"I don't 'care about' you, Clea. I love you."

I should leave it at that. I can see in his eyes it's true. But I can't.

"How? You've lost so much of what we had."

"You're wrong. I remember everything we've had." He takes my pizza and sets it down along with his own, then climbs behind me and rubs my shoulders. His big, strong hands feel so good on me, and I can feel his breath against my neck. "The first time we met, you chased me down through a jungle. I'd have gotten away, but you fell and got hurt, so I tried to help you . . . and you yelled at me."

I smile. "I thought you were stalking me."

"And yet you still took me on. Very ballsy. I was impressed."

"That's what you love?"

"That's what I found intriguing. I also remember you, me, Rayna, and Ben eating pizza in a crappy hotel near JFK. You wore purple sweatpants, your hair was in a ponytail, you had no makeup . . . and you were the most beautiful woman I'd ever seen."

"Hmm. When a man with memory loss says you're the most beautiful woman he's ever seen, I believe you have to take it with a grain of salt."

"I believe you're missing the point."

"Also, I'm pretty sure I was wearing a little mascara."

"I stand corrected." Sage kisses my neck, and I tilt my head all the way to the side, surrendering to his touch.

"I remember the beach in Japan," he says.

"I remember kissing you five minutes before I thought I would die, and I remember thinking that if all I did in my lifetime was make you, Clea Raymond, happy—even for a little while—it was enough."

I turn to face him and look into the eyes that have followed me forever. I wrap my arms around his waist and melt into him. Whatever he looks like on the outside, this is the man I want to be with for the rest of my life.

five

CLEA

The next week is a strange mix of wonderful and devastating. For the most part, spending time with Sage is everything I ever wanted. We stay in the house, but the hours we spend together are simple, easy, and fun. It's like I'm falling in love with Sage all over again, a Sage who looks different, but who proves every day that he's still my soulmate. And while he no longer has the memories of our past lifetimes together, every day we make new memories and grow even closer than before.

In so many ways I'm blissfully happy. There are just a few things that stand in the way.

The first, of course, is Rayna. I feel terrible that she doesn't know the truth, and the closer Sage and I get, the more I feel like I'm betraying her. I try to reach her every day. I call, I e-mail, I text, I write her letters begging her to give me ten minutes to just talk to her. . . . I even knock on her door when I know Wanda's out with the horses, but Rayna never responds. I'm so frustrated that I fantasize about dragging Sage to her doorstep and shocking her so badly she'll have to listen, but I'd never actually do it. Much as I want to talk to her face-to-face, I know that if she keeps refusing to see me, I'll have to write everything in a letter and send it to her. It's not perfect, and if anyone else sees what I wrote they'll think I'm certifiable, but it's less unfair than letting her live with half the story.

Another problem is with Sage. The memory lapses keep getting worse. He doesn't forget anything major, like who or where he is or who I am, but it's a constant string of little things. He'll restart a conversation that we just had an hour ago. Or he'll suggest that we see a movie we just saw the day before. When I point that out, he snaps at me. Horrible diatribes, calling me names and accusing me of holding him captive in the house. That's awful, but the anger never lasts long, so I focus on the good times and let the bad ones go. I write the memory lapses down in Ben's steno book, toning down the angry outbursts. No need to freak him out.

Ben meant it when he said he'd help. Every day he spends hours either in Dad's studio or in the Yale library going through the oldest books in their rare text archive, trying to find anything that might be relevant. When he's at the house, he takes the steno pages and adds them to his own ever-growing notebook. That's what he's flipping through now, as he, Sage, and I eat Chinese takeout at the kitchen island. With Piri gone, we're having a lot of takeout.

Sage has a spoonful of egg drop soup halfway to his mouth when he wheels on Ben. "Will you stop that? I'm not that interesting."

I tense up. So far Sage hasn't had an outburst in front of Ben. Is one coming now?

Ben stops scratching notes. "On the contrary, you're a fascinating man."

"You keep watching me. I feel like I'm in a zoo."

"More like house arrest," Ben says. I kick him under the table.

"Exactly," Sage agrees. "How about we go *out* for a change."

"We can't," I say. "What if someone sees you?"

"I'll wear a hat. I'll wear sunglasses. I'll wear a trench coat. We'll go far enough away that we won't run into Rayna or her mom."

I feel like he's on the edge. I won't push it by telling him the truth. It's not about him seeing Rayna and Wanda; it's about him having a memory lapse and running off with no way to get back to me, or slipping into a rage and doing who knows what. It's just safer to stay here, where even if he tried to slip out, the alarm system would let me know.

"Much as I'd love to see you in Bad Secret Agent Chic," Ben says, "I think I have an idea what's going on. Why you're having troubles after the soul transfer."

"You do?" I ask.

Ben looks from me to Sage. "What do you know about organ donation?"

"Why?" Sage asks. "Are you planning to give up a kidney?"

"Not at the moment. But when someone gets a new organ, the body can reject it. It *does* reject it, almost always, unless the patient takes drugs that stop the rejection."

"But Sage didn't get a new organ," I say.

"He didn't get *a* new organ," Ben says, "he got *all* new organs. And it almost didn't happen. Think about how many things had to line up for it to work. He had to be stabbed in the heart, at midnight, with a specific dagger that would rip his soul from his body."

"Funny," Sage says, shifting uncomfortably, "it sounds so pleasant when you describe it."

"Sorry. I'm just laying it out so you understand. Even after all that, the purpose of the dagger and the ceremony you went through was to drain the Elixir of Life from your body, and wrench your soul away from any kind of salvation. We heard all this from Magda, remember? Your soul was supposed to swirl around in eternal pain and agony until it dissolved into nothingness."

"You've really never considered a career as a poet?" Sage asks. "Maybe a grief counselor?"

"I swear I have a point. The Elixir is gone. That worked. We know because of your cut. You're mortal now. What didn't work is your soul getting wrenched away, and that's because there happened to be a host body right there that had just lost its own soul."

"Nico," I say.

Ben nods. "That body was there and empty, but it's not like it was planning to receive a new soul. It was dying. Sage's arrival was a shock to the system. Like a body getting an organ transplant. Only for an organ transplant, doctors prepare the patient with antirejection medicine."

"To suppress the immune system," I say. My dad had been a surgeon, so I know a little about this. "The body doesn't recognize the new organ as its own. It thinks it's a threat, and attacks it."

"Exactly," Ben says. "But Nico's body wasn't prepped, so the same way it might try to reject a donated organ, it might be trying to reject the new soul."

"That's impossible," I say. "An organ is concrete. You can hold it and measure it. A soul is . . . it's ephemeral. You can't pin it down. The body can't attack it, because there is no 'it' to attack."

Sage has been quiet, taking this in, but now he speaks in a measured voice. "Of course there is. The soul is its own entity. It has a life that goes beyond the body. The three of us should know that better than anyone."

"Are you sure?" I ask Ben. "You really think that's what's causing the . . . everything?"

"I'm not positive. It's not like there are medical journals on the topic. I'm extrapolating from stories and myths. But the symptoms are pretty consistent with everything he's going through: the sickness, the hunger, the blank spots . . . Yeah, I really think that's what's happening."

"So what can we do to change it?" I ask. "What's the spiritual equivalent of organ rejection drugs?"

"I haven't found one yet, but that doesn't mean it isn't there. So far I've just found the things that can go wrong with the transfer, but I'll keep looking. I've found references to other texts, at other libraries. . . . I'll find what we need."

Sage watches as Ben pushes his steamed shrimp and mixed vegetables around his plate. When he speaks, his voice is soothing.

"You already have. You know what comes next. If we don't find an antidote."

"I don't know anything for sure," Ben tells his plate.

"But . . ."

"They're old stories. And sometimes they're allegories, so you can't take them literally."

"Ben!" I say. "Stop stalling. Just tell us. Please."

Ben gives a long exhale, then speaks in a single breath. "The stories describe a descent into madness by the new body/soul combination, often including violence against himself and others . . . and ending in death."

"His own death?" I ask, my voice tinny in my ear.

"The struggling soul rarely goes down alone. There are usually other victims. Sometimes just one . . . sometimes many."

I feel like the air has been sucked out of the room, but Sage is calm. He leans back in his seat. "So now we know. How long do we have?"

"Not sure," Ben says.

"Then here's what we need to do, and I'm telling you both right now, because I won't be in a position to say it later, and because we've gotten into trouble with this kind of thing before. I don't want to be here if I'm a danger to the people around me. When things get bad, one of you needs to do something about it."

"What are you saying?" I ask. "You think we're going to *kill* you?"

Sage's response is simple. "Do you love me?"

"What kind of a question is that? Of course I do! If I didn't, I—"

"If you love me, you won't let me become a monster."

My mouth is open, ready to scream back at

him, but instead I just shake my head. "I can't."

"So it's up to you," Sage says to Ben.

"I won't. I can't." His voice cracks. "I already have blood on my hands. I can't do it again."

"Okay," Sage says. "How about this: Lock me up. When it gets to the point where I can't control myself, have me committed. Then I can't hurt anyone."

"That I can do," Ben says.

"Good." They shake on it like boys making a trade in a school yard, and my head all but explodes.

"Stop! What are you doing? This is your life we're talking about!"

"Yes, it is," Sage says, as if that puts a period on the argument.

"But Ben said he's basing this stuff on stories that aren't even real. He has no idea if this will happen."

"And I have confidence you won't put me in a padded cell and straitjacket unless it's absolutely necessary."

"You're *joking* about this?"

"No, I'm not," he says, so matter-of-fact that I want to smack him. He holds up his wrist. The bandages are gone now, but there's still a thick scar from where the beer bottle sliced him open. "When I got this, you know what it meant to me?"

"That you could die?"

"No. That I could *live*. This proves the Elixir is gone. I don't have eternal life. I don't have anything anyone else wants. When I look at it, I know no one's coming after us, and we can live like normal people. That's what I want, Clea. I want to live with you, and grow old with you, and one day, a long, long, *long* time from now, I want to die with you, knowing our souls will be together for whatever comes next."

"That's what I want too," I say.

"Then we'll fight for it, and we'll hold on tight to every second we have. But if we can't have that future, if I can't have the life I want, I refuse to take you down with me. That would be worse than dying."

Tears fill my eyes, but I won't give in. "It won't happen. You won't get any worse."

"Ben?" he asks.

"I'll take care of it," Ben says quietly. "If it comes to that."

Before Ben goes home, he and Sage exchange a very formal handshake, then I hug Ben tightly. "Find a cure," I say in his ear. "We have to."

"We will."

Ben's prognosis scares me, but I'm not convinced it's inevitable. Old myths and stories aren't always true. Nico's body and Sage's soul have gone through serious trauma, and it only makes sense that they both need time to heal. The memory lapses aren't a sign of worse things to come, they're bumps on the road to health.

Still, they make me think of my own memories of Sage's and my history, and how they might fade. I don't dream about my past lives anymore, and part of me mourns the loss of the women I used to be. I start writing down everything I remember about them, and I promise the memory of Olivia that one day, when Sage is healthy and Rayna knows the truth and has forgiven us, Sage and I will go to Italy and have the wedding she was promised, but never got to enjoy.

I also write about the way Sage used to look. At this point it's his new face and body that I see when I close my eyes and think about him. His gestures, posture, and soulful eyes don't look like they're hanging out on someone else's body anymore. They look like they belong.

I have the man I've always wanted, but I still wish I had some relic of the man he used to be.

Then I realize I could.

The next day I wait until Sage is asleep and call a store that usually doesn't deliver, but they agree when I offer to pay double. I make sure Sage and I are upstairs when the guy arrives, and fly downstairs before he can catch up and see what I'm getting. I quickly pop the plastic bag from the store into a backpack, so Sage won't know what it is right away.

He's staring out the window when I come in. "Who was at the door?"

"Delivery. I have a surprise for you."

He smiles wickedly. "Will I like it?"

"I think you'll like it very much, but first I have to ask you a question. When you imagine yourself, do you see yourself in this body?"

Sage looks surprised, but he thinks it over. "The truth? No. Every time I look in the mirror I'm surprised . . . which is probably why I avoid looking in the mirror as much as I can."

"Good."

"Good?" Sage laughs. "Why? Did I spend too much time gazing at myself before?"

"No. It's just . . . I want the chance to see what you see." I plop down on the floor, open up the backpack, and pull out everything I'd had delivered from the art supply store: charcoal sticks and pencils, a pad of paper, kneaded erasers, and a foam brush. I lay each element out on the carpet, one by one.

"Draw yourself. The way you see yourself when you close your eyes."

Sage is the most talented artist I've ever known, but he hasn't drawn at all since he's been back. I know he'll be excited for the chance, and I eagerly watch his face for the smile I'm sure is coming . . . but instead he looks at me like I broke his heart.

"What's wrong?" I ask. "Did I get the wrong stuff? The guy on the phone said charcoals are perfect for faces. Would paint have been better?"

Sage shakes his head. The muscles in his jaw clench and unclench, and he won't meet my eyes. Panic swirls inside me.

"Sage, talk to me! What is it?"

I get up and sit next to him, but he shifts away so I can't touch him.

"This is who I am, Clea," he says through clenched teeth. "This face. This body. I thought you understood. I thought you were okay with that."

"I do. I am. I know who you are, Sage. I just—"

Again I reach for him, but he leans back on his

hands and turns away to stare out the window. His eyes look tortured.

"I'm sorry, Sage. I'm so sorry. I didn't mean . . ."

"You look at me, but you don't see me at all."

"That's not true."

"I'm like a substitute for a man who doesn't exist anymore. Even if we get a lifetime together, you'll always feel like there's something missing. Always."

"No! Sage, you're wrong." I rush to stash the art supplies in the backpack, desperate to turn back the clock and undo my mistake. "This was a stupid idea. I don't know what I was thinking."

"I do," Sage says.

He stalks out of the room. His legs are so long I need to trot to keep up with him. "What are you doing? Sage, talk to me!"

I reach out and grab his wrist, but he gives his arm a fierce twist to shake me off. I chase him through the house to the foyer, where he grabs my car keys from their hook.

"No! Sage, you can't leave!"

I lunge and grab him tightly now, pulling back on his arm. "You can't go out there! What if some-one sees? What if —"

"Let me *go*!" He pushes the middle of my chest

with his free arm, so hard that I sprawl backward, completely out of control, and slam into the wall. There's a low shelf mounted there and my head slams hard, biting into its edge. I crumple to the floor, but I'm glad because Sage has never been this violent, and the sight of what he just did will shock him out of this. . . .

But he doesn't even look at me, just stalks outside.

Thank God I was too excited about the art supplies to reset the alarm, I think. *That would bring Wanda running. Maybe Rayna too.*

I hear my car start up and squeal away.

Let him at least drive far, so no one Nico knows sees him, I think, then feel immediately guilty, because who knows what kind of trouble Sage could get into driving around in a rage? *Forget that. . . . Just let him be safe.*

I reach to the back of my head, and my fingers come back slicked with blood.

Shit.

I get to my feet slowly, and when I know I'm not light-headed, I stagger to the closet and grab a clean washcloth, which I fill with ice and press onto my cut. I stare at myself in the hall mirror and check my pupils to make sure they're dilating normally. Everything seems fine — no concussion — so I lie down on the couch, the iced cloth keeping pressure on my head.

I should have known. How did I feel when I thought Sage looked at me and saw one of my other lives? I hated it. I felt rejected, like I was nothing but a fallback — the closest thing he could get to the woman he loved, but not her. And I felt that way even without Sage doing anything as stupid and callous as asking me to draw a picture of myself the way I was before.

I am a horrible human being.

I wince at my own thoughts. I sound like a battered girlfriend, making excuses and blaming myself.

This is different, though. Yes, a battered girlfriend would say that, too, but this really is. Sage would never hurt me if he was in his right mind. And okay, maybe that's an excuse, but it's not like he hurts me all the time. It happened once. Who says it'll ever happen again? And if it does . . . it's not like I'd make excuses for him forever.

Would I?

I can't think about it. It's such a mind knot. I'm not that girl who puts up with whatever her boyfriend dishes out because she knows he loves her. I would never be that girl.

But I'd also never turn away from Sage.

It doesn't matter. What matters is that Sage is out there in the world and he's not thinking clearly. He could do anything. He could get hurt. Any minute now, the police could knock on my door and tell me there's been a horrible accident. What am I supposed to do, just sit here with ice on my head and wait for it to happen? Maybe I should take my mom's car and try to find him.

Except I have no idea where he went. I don't even know what direction he turned when he left the property. There'd be a one-in-a-million chance that I'd find him. Better for me to wait and be here when he comes back.

If he comes back.

He'll come back. And when he does, we'll get him well.

No, I'll get him well *now*. I'll do research. I have a different perspective from Ben; maybe I'll find something he missed. I'm still bleeding a little, so instead of going to the computer, I pull out my cell phone and Google "mythology soul transfers."

The search returns "about 21,300,000 results,"

and none of the top hits have anything to do with Sage's situation.

So much for my fresh perspective; the Internet is no help at all.

Now what?

All I can do is wait.

By sunset I've chewed every one of my fingernails down to the quick, and I'm pacing the house in a panic. When my cell phone rings with a stranger's last name on the ID, I'm positive it's someone who found Sage's car wrapped around a tree and heard my number as Sage recited it with his last breath. . . .

"Hello?"

"Clea . . . it's me."

"Where are you? Are you okay?"

"I'm fine, but . . . I don't know where I am. I don't know how I got here. I borrowed someone's phone. Maybe she can tell you where I am. . . ."

At the word "her" I imagine some gorgeous siren taking advantage of the hot amnesiac wandering the streets, but the woman's voice sounds at least eighty years old.

"Are you Clea?" she asks. "This young man seems to be lost."

"I know. Can you tell me where you are?"

"He's here at the diner. Wandered in looking sad and confused."

"Yes. *Which* diner?"

"Attached to the bowling alley. It's a slow night, no league play, otherwise I never would have had the time to chat with your young man. He ordered a piece of pie and some coffee, and the minute I served it up, I said to myself, 'Enid, something with this boy isn't quite right.'"

If I could reach through the phone and grab the information out of her, I would. I struggle not to scream and ask, "Please, just . . . *Where* is the diner? Can you give me the address?"

She does. Sage is in Rhode Island less than two hours away, so he wasn't driving the entire time he was gone. I get the address and promise to get there as soon as I can.

"You do that," Enid says. "And be sure to bring a couple dollars. He doesn't have a wallet with him, and I mentioned he had some coffee and pie, right?"

"Yes, you did," I say, grabbing a jacket and my mom's car keys. "I'll pay for it."

I hang up before she can say anything else, then program the address into Mom's navigation system. An hour and a half later, I pull up to Min's

Pins, a decrepit bowling alley with a half-lit neon sign. I can see into the attached glass-walled diner. The only one at the counter is Sage, his shoulders slouched over an untouched soup and sandwich. An octogenarian in a uniform that looks like a French maid outfit bustles between him and the three couples sitting in the booths. That must be Enid.

My car isn't in the parking lot.

I run inside, and the look of despair on Sage's face when he sees me breaks my heart. I take his face and kiss him, feel the stubble against my skin.

"Hi," he says. "I'm so sorry."

The lump on the back of my head throbs a little as I think about it. "You remember?"

He shakes his head sadly. "I don't really know how I got here. I'm so sorry. And I love you. I just . . ."

He's searching for the lost time, I can see it in his face. But it's hopeless.

"Don't worry," I say. "It's okay."

"No, it's not."

"Let's go home."

I pull his hands into mine and rub my fingers over his knuckles until he slides off the stool and wraps an arm over my shoulders. "You deserve better than this, Clea."

"Hey, lovebirds," Enid calls. "The check?"

I pay it, then lead Sage outside.

"I'm guessing you don't know where my car is?"

He shakes his head. "I'm sorry."

"It's okay. I can report it stolen tomorrow. Someone will find it."

We get into my mom's car and start the long drive home. Neither of us says anything for a while. We just sit in the dark, the streetlights washing over us.

"I'm an ass," he finally says.

The back of my head throbs as we go over a bump in the road. "What's the last thing you remember?"

"You asked for a picture, I jumped down your throat. I guess I left the house after that?"

"You did. But it's my fault. I shouldn't have asked. It was stupid of me. I know you love to draw, and I was trying to be sweet, but I should have realized you'd get upset. I'm so sorry. This is all my fault."

"No, it's not. Of course you're going to think about what I was before. It makes sense."

"But I don't. I mean, yes, I think about it, but I don't wish for it. I don't pine for it. I wanted the picture as a memory of what *was*. But when I think about what *is*, what I want for the rest of my life . . . I think about you, exactly the way you are right now."

"You don't wish things were different? You don't miss the romance of a man who'd live forever and follow you lifetime after lifetime?"

I can't believe it. He's insecure, something I never thought I'd see in Sage. There hasn't been one second I wished he was still immortal, but he's afraid of it. I glance to the side and see it in his eyes, the way his face looks so boyish and vulnerable.

"Sage, I love you. *You*. I don't care what you look like, and I don't need you to be anything but who you are. I promise."

I reach for his hand and squeeze it, then count the minutes until we get home and I can wrap myself around him. We kiss once we stop in the driveway, but I cut it short because I don't want to be discovered. It's torture to break away from him for even the few seconds it takes to get into the house. Once we're inside, I throw myself back into his arms, but he gently pushes me away.

"There's something I want to do. I just need a few minutes."

I'm instantly afraid for him. He'd rather hurt himself than hurt me. But then I remember he doesn't know he slammed me into a wall. Still . . .

"Are you okay?" I ask.

"I'm fine. I promise. I just need a little while, that's all."

What can I do but trust him?

"Okay," I say. "I'll take a shower."

I spend a long time under the water, luxuriating in the hot stream against my skin. When I'm done, I wrap up in a thick terry robe and pad to my room . . . where I see a large piece of paper sitting on my comforter. I walk closer to check it out: It's a beautiful charcoal, a picture of me and Sage—*my* Sage, the one I always knew. We're curled up together at the beach . . . maybe the beach in Japan, but it doesn't look quite like that. He's stretched out on his side, I'm leaning against him. My camera's in one hand, and I look out at the waves as if framing the perfect photograph in my mind.

Scrawled on the bottom of the picture are the words: *It's good to remember. I love you.*

"Do you like it?"

I turn around and he's there, just as much the man of my dreams as the one in the picture.

"I love it. And I love you."

I walk into his arms and kiss him, and I'm so lost in the moment I don't even know there's anything else in this world until I hear the choking scream.

"NICO?"

The voice rings out like a gunshot, and Sage and I spring apart and turn to the door.

Oh my God.

It's Rayna.

six

RAYNA

When I first heard about Nico, I thought I'd lie in bed and cry forever.

I didn't.

At some point I stopped, but I don't know when. I'm in a total fog. I don't know if it's been a minute or a week that I've been lying here.

Maybe not a week.

I think I fell asleep. There's light coming in my window. My throat is dry, and it hurts to swallow. I'm still clutching at my pillows. I must have been squeezing them in my sleep. I have to concentrate to get my arms to relax away from them, and when I do, my muscles are so stiff they scream. My eyelids weigh a ton apiece, and my face moves like a starched collar.

I also have to pee, which I would have done before now if I'd really been in bed a week, so it's probably been less than that. Maybe even less than a day.

I stare at my wall. I have seen every episode of *Hoarders* and I am not a hoarder . . . except on my walls. When I was three years old, my mom said my bedroom was mine and I could decorate it any way I wanted. "Within reason," she said. She vetoed my seventh-birthday plan of turning it into a safari complete with real live elephants. I bet if I'd wanted horses, she'd have let me.

Since then, I've taped everything that interested me on my walls: articles, pictures, posters, movie stubs, small objects . . . everything. And I never take any of it down; I just add layers. It's like living inside a scrapbook, or a Pinterest page. The newest stuff is the Nico section. To plan it out, I lay in bed and scoped out the wall from there so I'd be sure to mount everything at exact first-thing-in-the-morning eye level. It was a great idea at the time, but it sucks right now. I stare at every picture I snapped of him and us with my cell phone, the handkerchief he gave me when I sneezed (A handkerchief. Seriously. How cute is that?), and even an extra sugar cube from the pile he gave me to feed the horses. My mom thinks a sugar cube on the wall will bring ants, but I put enough tape on it that it's basically laminated, so it's all good.

My favorite of all the pictures is the one I printed out largest, an eight-by-ten of Nico in the door frame of the stables. I always laugh when I see it. His arm is cocked up, the forearm leaning against the jamb, and the pose and his muscular body make him look like a model, but with an entirely un-model-like dorky grin that I should absolutely not find sexy, but I can't help it, I do.

He's such an earnest goofball.

I don't even realize I'm crying again until I feel the tears drip from my numb cheeks onto my arm, but then I can't stop, and pretty soon I'm sobbing and coughing again, pulling the pillows back into my arms until at some point I fall back asleep.

Maybe I will stay in bed forever. Or at least a week. Maybe when you hurt this much, your body stops needing to do things like pee.

Maybe not. The next time I open my eyes it's

dark again outside, and I either have to move or
wet myself. I waffle about it for a while, but since
I can't possibly stay bedridden on a wet mattress,
I stagger out into the hall. Weird how one horrible
day can turn around years of yoga. Not only am I
no longer one with my body, it and I aren't even
speaking the same language. My limbs are glued
in place, and my brain is detached and floating
several feet away, trying to find any kind of path
back to Nico.

Mom's there when I get out of the bathroom.
She's dressed in her elasticized jeans and one of
the mountainous button-down plaid cotton shirts
she likes to wear over a scoop-necked tee when
she works. She doesn't say anything when she
sees me, just wraps me in a huge hug that's maybe
a minute away from becoming Suffocation by
Breast.

Dad must have called her cell to tell her I was
awake. She smells like the stables. Like Nico. I
start crying all over again.

"What happened, baby?" She coos the way she
did when I was five and fell out of the climbing
tree in our backyard. "Whatever it is, we'll make
it better, okay?"

"We can't," I croak.

"I can try," she promises. "But you need to talk to me."

I can't say it. I cry until my body feels like it's ripping apart, and I'm so grateful to Mom that she doesn't try to coax it out of me anymore.

"Shhh, baby. Shhh. It's okay. Everything is okay."

She bends down and sweeps her arm under my knees, scooping me into a fireman's carry like I'm a little girl again, and carries me to bed. I fall asleep while she's rubbing my back, and when I wake up she's there again, but her clothes have changed and the sun shines in my window, so I must have slept through the night.

There are tears in her eyes, and I bolt upright. "Mom?"

"Oh, baby, I'm so sorry."

"Did Clea tell you?" I haven't used my voice in a while. It's raspy.

Mom shakes her head. "I don't poke my head in when you girls fight. And she didn't have to tell me. I went to his house." She didn't have to say his name. She knew I'd know who she meant. "He didn't show up for work, so I went by his apartment. I thought something happened between the two of you, and I was all set to yell at him for letting that get in the way of his job." She gives a low, rueful laugh that turns into the littlest sob. "Some friends of his were there, packing his things to ship back to his mother."

"Did they say what happened?" I whisper the question, not positive I want to know the details.

Mom shakes her head. "You know, Clea's been calling a lot. Coming to the house, too. I told her to stop. I said you'd find her whenever you're ready."

"Thanks, Mom."

"Baby, I don't know what went on between the two of you, but it seems to me like now's a really good time to have your best friend by your side."

She means well, but she doesn't get it. She can't get it, and there's no good way for me to explain it, so I just stay silent.

"Whatever you need," Mom says. She stays in the room until I fall asleep again.

The next few days are surreal. I don't go to school, but Mom takes care of it. She tells my high school there are "extenuating circumstances" and makes it clear that she'll kick their butts if they give her a hard time about me missing as much time as I need, so they don't. They probably don't care that much, since it's April of my senior year and the whole college application thing is a done deal. I already got acceptance letters from a couple of fallback schools, though I can't imagine going anywhere beyond my bedroom and the bathroom, maybe ever. I wear the same yoga pants and soft baby tee until they practically jump off me and walk themselves to the laundry, at which point I put on the same outfit in another color. It doesn't matter; I'm not leaving the house.

Clea calls a zillion times a day. And texts. And e-mails. I just ignore them. I ignore Ben, too. He calls a bunch and says it's important, but I know it's not. The only important thing is that Nico's gone.

Mom got a call from Nico's mother. I guess Nico really did ask his mom for his grandmother's ring, because she had our information and apparently knows all about me. She called to tell my mom there's going to be a funeral, back in Montana. I'm invited to the service, but I don't want to go. I tell Mom I have no desire to see Nico's body in a coffin.

"That's the strange thing," Mom says. It's late, long after her phone call with Nico's mother, and she's wrapped in her robe. She and I both sit on the bed and stare at the TV. I like to keep it on, as long as it's nothing too dramatic. Even my standby reality TV has had too much emotion lately, so I've been watching game shows. The old episodes of *Match Game* and *$25,000 Pyramid* are my favorites; lots of sixties and seventies fashions to check out. If I were ever leaving the house, I'd want a pair of Brett Somers's sunglasses.

Mom likes to join me here in the evenings. Dad visits too—he brings my dinner up on a tray. He never says much, just pats me on my arm before he leaves the room to go downstairs and eats with Mom, then Mom comes up for dessert. Tonight we're sharing a plate of brownies and staring at an episode of *Family Feud* from sometime in the eighties, where Richard Dawson is making out with every woman on the show.

"What's the strange thing?" I ask. I assume it's some weird kind of custom you do when your family's part of a bizarro cult and people die a lot.

"I asked if the funeral would be open casket. I thought you'd want to know if you were going. She said no . . . because they don't have his body."

Something prickles over my skin, and I sit up straighter. "Why not?"

"She said it wasn't found."

"I don't understand. How do they know he's dead?"

"Believe me, I asked. She said they spoke to enough people who were there when it happened— whatever exactly happened—and they know." Mom reaches over and strokes my hair back from my forehead. "So what I'm saying, baby, is that if you do want to go, you won't have to see anything you don't want to see."

"That's okay," I say. "I still don't want to go."

I'm speaking, but my nerves are on fire and my mind is a million miles away.

There is no body.

Does that mean Nico could be alive?

His family doesn't think so, but with everyone dying so young, his family must be all kinds of messed up, right? Nico expected to die by the time he was thirty; they must have thought so too. They were probably *waiting* for a call that he was dead. Hell, Nico probably could have called *himself* and said he'd died and they would have believed him.

He might still be alive. He might.

"Rayna? Did you hear me?"

Oops. Mom said something.

"Sorry. Zoned out for a second."

"Rayna." Mom looks deep into my eyes, as if trying to read my thoughts. She does a pretty great job of it too. "His mother *did* talk to people who were there. She didn't go into detail, but she made it very clear that he's really gone."

"I understand," I say, by which I mean that I understand his mother *thinks* he's really gone, but she's almost 100 percent certainly wrong. I try to keep my thoughts a secret, but I suck at that kind of thing, and it doesn't help that I suddenly can't sit still. I jounce my knees up and down and drum my fingers on the mattress. Mom looks sad, and I know she doesn't want to see me get my hopes up for nothing, but she doesn't know the whole story, and there's no way I can explain it.

I jump out of bed and get into Mountain Pose, then do some Breath of Fire to let out the energy swirling through my body. Thirty seconds of superfast, super-deep inhalations, in through the nose and out through the mouth, fully inflating and deflating my abdomen each time. From there I take a long, deep cleansing breath to get me centered and focused.

It works. I know exactly what I have to do. I sniff at my T-shirt and decide it's decent enough, then go to my closet and pull on a hoodie.

"I have to go see Clea," I tell Mom, and I'm halfway out the door when she stops me.

"Wait, baby," she says. "There's one more thing."

"Now?" I whine like an impatient child and bounce on my toes.

"I found something today. In the stables. You know the little desk we have in there? It was tucked in the back of the drawer. I imagine he wanted to surprise you there."

I immediately stop bouncing. "Surprise me with what?"

"I almost didn't show you," Mom admits. "I don't want anything to make it worse. But it's for you, so it's your right to have it."

She reaches into her robe pocket and pulls out a small box wrapped in plain white paper. Scrawled on top of the box in Nico's handwriting is my name and a message. *To Rayna*, it says, *One Day . . .* Looking at his loopy print makes my heart hurt with anticipation. He's alive. I'll see him again. I'm sure of it, and whatever's in this box is just something to tide me over until it happens. I tear off the wrapper to find a completely nondescript cardboard box, the kind you'd buy at Office Depot.

I take off the top, and my heart stops.

A ring. Is it his grandmother's wedding ring? But before he left he said he didn't have it yet, that his mom was going to send it.

I spill the ring into my palm. This is no wedding ring, and it did *not* belong to a woman. It's huge — a thick gold band with a raised engraving of three swirls, each growing out of the same central spot. The swirls are surrounded by a thick outer circle in gold.

One Day, the box said. It sounds like a message for a promise ring — exactly the kind of thing he wanted to give me. I try to slip the ring onto my thumb, but even that's too thin by half to fit the wide circle. Did he maybe think this was the ring he wanted, and only later realize it would be enormous on me? It *is* the sort of ridiculously cute thing he'd do, but come on, did he honestly think my fingers were anywhere near this thick?

Mom's apparently thinking the same thing.

"Maybe he meant it to be a necklace," she says. "Or a paperweight."

Paperweight probably not so much, but I head to my wall, where a series of hooks poke out from among the collage of random keepsakes, each one dripping with a tangle of necklaces and brace-

lets. I detach an empty gold chain from one of the
hooks and string it through the ring, which drops
like a lead weight.

My new necklace might be heavy, but I've
never felt lighter. I bounce to the side of the bed,
hand the chain to Mom, and spin around, lifting
my hair so she can clasp it around my neck.

"You sure you don't want to use it as a paperweight?" she asks as the ring thumps against my
chest. "You'll get backaches wearing this around.
It's enormous."

I drop the ring under my T-shirt so I can feel
it against my heart. Or maybe not—I think your
heart is on the left side, and the ring falls pretty
squarely in upper-cleavage land, but it's way more
romantic to imagine it against my heart, so I'm
going with that. It *is* heavy, but I'm only wearing
it until Nico and I are back together again. Then
he can wear it, and I'll wear his grandmother's
ring when his mom sends it. Hopefully she won't
do anything crazy like get rid of that ring now
that she thinks he's gone, or bury it in his honor
or something. No worries—if she does, we'll get
another made instead. One just like the behemoth
around my neck, but small and delicate.

I spin back around to face Mom. "Thank you,"

I say, and kiss her on the cheek. "I'll be back. I'm going to go see Clea."

I run downstairs and stop by the selection of keys hanging on small hooks by the front door. Mom is the key master—she has copies of keys to everything on the property, from the stables, to the cars, to the ancient wood box full of tennis equipment. She used to keep them all in a lockbox . . . until she lost the key to it. Now they're out in the open, but there are so many, and they're labeled in such a random way, that even if a thief did manage to get past the outer gates and alarm system and into our house, he'd never know what to do with them.

I don't have that issue; I know most of the keys by sight. I grab the one to Clea's place, then sprint across to her front door. As I use the key to let myself in and climb the steps to Clea's room, I think about how Clea told me the news about Nico. She never said she saw a body. What did she see to make her believe Nico was dead? She must believe it—there's no way she'd tell me Nico was gone if she didn't think it was true. No matter how mad at her I've been, I know she wouldn't do that to me. I need to know everything she saw. Then we can figure out what really happened, where Nico is right now, and why he hasn't come back for me, which he would unless he was hurt . . . or had amnesia.

I'm going with amnesia. It's so romance novel. He has amnesia, and he's wandering the streets somewhere . . . or maybe he's hurt *and* has amnesia, and he's in a hospital somewhere thinking he's someone else entirely, but I'll find him, and my mere presence will bring back his memories little by little. . . .

Yes. That's how it's going to happen. I'll find him. Clea will help me. I was awful to her, but I was so hurt. She'll understand, and we'll work together to track down Nico. Sage can help too. And Ben. Hell, we can even bring Suzanne, so Ben has someone. It'll be an adventure, and it'll end like a romantic comedy, with all of us paired off with the perfect person for each of us.

Clea's bedroom door is wide open, so I run inside . . . but I can't make sense of what I see. Even when it comes together, it doesn't click. I only know there's molten lava filling my stomach and I want to be sick.

It's Clea, and she's wrapped in someone's arms,

and they're kissing like they can't get enough of each other. . . .

But the man she's kissing isn't Sage.

"NICO?"

The two of them spring apart and turn to face me. They're bookends of shock.

"Oh no," Clea says. She jumps between Nico and me as if she could hide him with her body. "Rayna, it's not what you think."

"Really? What are you doing? You told me he was dead!"

"I know I did, and I wasn't lying—"

"He's right in front of me, Clea!"

She's still standing in front of him, like she's guarding him. Clea's the one who needs guarding. I'm pacing in front of her like a pitbull waiting for the right moment to spring, and I'm ready to draw blood.

"I *knew* he was alive. That's why I came over. I *knew* it! But stupid me, I thought you *didn't* know. I thought you made a mistake and you'd be so happy to help me find him once you knew he was alive because you're my *best . . . freaking . . . friend!* What are you doing, Clea?"

I attack her as I scream. I grab her arms and

shake her, digging my nails into her flesh. It feels good, but it's not enough until I swing back and land the perfect slap right across her face.

"Stop it!" Nico cries.

"Oh, you're going to take her side? I *hate* you! I've been a mess for days! I haven't left my bed! What kind of crazy assholes come up with *death* to cover up cheating? Your mother is having a *funeral* for you!"

"My mother? You don't know what you're talking about."

"You told me you loved me! I'm wearing your stupid-ass ring." I tug it toward him, brandishing it in front of me. "'One Day,' you said. Were you two already together? Or is that what it meant, '*One day* I'll be screwing your best friend'?"

Nico just stands there, his arms crossed, his face cold and stormy. I can't believe it. It's like he doesn't even care I'm here.

"You're out of control," he says matter-of-factly.

"*I'm* out of control? You said you wanted to *marry* me!" I lunge for him, but Clea jumps in front of me, pushing me back.

"Stop!" she says. "You don't understand!"

"Get off me!" Clea has her hands on my shoulders, so I reach out and grab a fistful of her blond hair. I tug until a clump rips free in my hands, and I laugh when Clea screams and drops to the floor.

"Get away from her!" Nico growls to me.

"Stop defending her!"

Without Clea in my way, I storm to Nico and beat on him again and again and again. I know I'm not hurting him — he's a tank — but I just want to have some effect on him, make him say or do *something*, even acknowledge what he did. But all he does is stand there and say in a voice as cold as ice, "Cut it out."

"No! I won't! You lied to me!"

"Stop it!"

"No!"

"I said *STOP IT!*"

Searing pain as he catches my fists in his hands and squeezes, hard. My fingernails pierce into my palms and my bones feel like they're crushed. I look up at Nico, and there's nothing but blank darkness in his eyes.

His eyes.

His brown eyes?

The pain is unbearable, and I collapse to the

ground, but he doesn't stop squeezing. The world is getting fuzzy, but I see Clea stagger upright and hurl herself at Nico. She grabs his arm and screams, "Sage! Stop it! Let go of her! *Sage!*"

Sage . . . Sage is inside Nico's body. . . . But how . . . ?

Darkness.

seven

CLEA

"Rayna . . . Rayna?"

She's unconscious on the ground, and I can't believe Sage did this to her. I don't even know if *he* believes it, or remembers it, or even knows he did it. He plopped down on the bed when Rayna collapsed, and he's still there, staring into nothingness.

"Rayna, please be okay. . . . Rayna?"

Her eyes flutter open, and she winces. "My hands . . ."

"Can you move them? Are they broken? Try to open and close your fist."

Slowly, she brings her fingers in and out. I can see the bloody crescents where her nails dug into her palm, but the bones aren't broken.

"You called him Sage," she says.

I nod.

"How?"

I start to tell her everything, picking up from when Nico, Ben, and I left her, but she's distracted. She keeps darting her eyes to Sage, and every time it's the same: She looks over, lights up with hope for the briefest of seconds despite herself, then remembers all over again that it's not him and sniffs away the tears. Sage is oblivious. I'm not even sure he's back to himself. At the risk of setting him off again, I sit next to him on the bed.

"Sage, maybe now would be a good time to rest."

"Yeah . . . yeah, I think it would."

He lies across the bed, but I stop him with, "I was thinking maybe in the spare bedroom. Alone."

I say it gently, and grit my teeth for the snap, but it doesn't happen. He just stops himself halfway to the pillow and changes direction, rising to his feet. He bends down to kiss me good night, but I give my head the smallest shake and he backs away with a sheepish half smile. "Good night," he says. "I'm—I—"

Is he going to apologize? Does he realize there's a reason to apologize?

"Good night," he says again after a long, deep sigh. He waves as he heads out of the room. Rayna watches him go, her eyes soaking in every movement and gesture.

"It's so weird," she says solemnly. "It's him, but it's not him at all. If I didn't know better, I'd think you found his long-lost twin."

"I'm glad you see it too," I admit. "Sometimes I think I want to see Sage so badly that I worry I'm projecting."

"You think you can project a whole new pair of eyes?"

"You noticed?"

A cloud drops over Rayna's face. "Yes, Clea, I noticed that the man I love has completely different-colored eyes from the last time I saw him. Is that so bizarre to you? Do you really think you're the only person in the world who would notice something like that?"

"Of course not."

"I think you do. I think you believe no one but you and Sage can truly love each other in a life-altering way."

"That's not true."

I say it, but in a way she's right. Not about Sage and me being the only ones to have an all-encompassing love, but maybe about assuming her connection with Nico wasn't as deep and meaningful as she said it was. I've known her since birth. She met her first "love of her life" when she was three years old—a blond boy named Alexander in our class at preschool. Even then she swore it was forever, and huffed and tossed her mop of red curls whenever anyone belittled it as "puppy love." For Rayna, falling in love is like breathing—she can't live without it.

Did it seem like she was particularly connected with Nico? Sure. But the two of them had only been together about a month. And yes, a month was a pretty good run for Rayna, but Owen, her junior-year boyfriend, had lasted *six* months. She was so sure she'd end up with Jackson, her longest-term boyfriend after that, she dragged him to an astrologist to figure out the most auspicious post-high-school wedding date.

That was two weeks before she stormed into my room freaking out because Jackson liked to rub his stocking feet together when he studied, and the *shush-shush* noise was making her rip her hair out and she *refused* to be bald by eighteen.

Were Rayna and Nico really soulmates? If he'd lived, would they have stayed together forever?

I don't know. And the truth is, it doesn't matter. Rayna believes it, and if I'm really her friend, that should be all I need.

"Life isn't all about Clea Raymond," she mutters. "The rest of us aren't extras here to fill in your life story."

"I never said you were."

"You didn't have to. It's how you live."

"It's not! Rayna, it killed me when you wouldn't talk to me, and not just because of the massive lie it left between us. That was awful, but worse was you not being in my life. We say the men we love are our soulmates, and maybe they are, but if anyone in this world is part of my soul, it's you. You're more than my best friend. You're my sister. You're more than my sister, even. You're a part of me, and I'm so sorry if I've ever made you think you're anything less."

Rayna doesn't say anything to me for a while, but then she smiles.

"That was good," she says. "Where'd you read that?"

"Shut. Up."

"*Cosmo*? It was *Cosmo*, wasn't it?"

"Rayna!"

"Okay, just hug me and get all the drama over with. I've been crying for a whole week. If I have to cry any more, I'll get massively dehydrated and have to go on IV fluids and my mom will go apeshit, and you know none of us want that."

She's waving her hands over her eyes to stop the tears, and I laugh and cry and throw my arms around her. I only pull out of the hug halfway, though—I keep my hands on her shoulders and my forehead against hers.

"One more thing," I say. "I'm *not* glad it was Nico who died and not Sage. That's not a choice I would ever make."

"I know," she says. "I knew it even when I said it, really. But thanks."

We sit there, head to head for another moment, then pull apart. Rayna takes a deep breath. "Keep telling me the story."

I do what she asks. I tell her how Ben led us to where Sage was being held; how Nico had the chance to kill Sage and end the curse plaguing his family and the rest of Cursed Vengeance, the other descendants of the original Elixir of Life thieves; how he hesitated just long enough for Ben to tackle him away from Sage; and how Nico landed on the dagger that took his life. I tell her another CV member didn't hesitate — she grabbed the dagger at the last possible second and plunged it into Sage's heart, ripping out his soul. She drained him of Elixir and wanted to drink it herself, but didn't get the chance before an otherworldly earthquake shook the Elixir out of her grip and sent it back into the ground. My voice chokes as I tell her how it felt to see Sage's body, dead on the altar. How I held him in the middle of the warscape, surrounded by the dead and injured, and how I thought I might die right there with him.

"That's horrible," Rayna says, and I know she means it, but the truth is, this story ends better for me than for her. That's what I tell her next: how the impossible happened. Nico rose from the ground, a dead man who lifted his shirt and healed right in front of us . . . but with a new soul inside.

"It was what Magda, the old woman we met in Shibuya, had said could happen," I tell her. "A soul transfer. A homeless soul finding refuge in a body whose soul had just recently moved on."

"Moved on," Rayna intones it like a prayer. "Is that really what happened? Is he somewhere better?"

I want to say yes, but I'm not going to lie. "I wish I knew. I'd like to think so, but I'm not really good with the heaven/hell/God/afterlife thing. I'm just not sure."

"Seriously? You're still a skeptic? *You?* What do you need, a burning bush? Maybe a pair of tablets falling down from your ceiling?"

"I'm not completely dense," I retort. "I get that there's *something*. There's a soul. It moves on, or it doesn't move on, or it comes back. I just don't know what's behind it all, if anything. Maybe there isn't. Maybe it's all just random. Maybe moving on is like everything you ever wanted coming true. Or maybe it's just . . . ending."

"Thanks. That makes me feel much better about Nico."

"I'm sorry. I swear I'm not trying to make it worse. I'm just being honest."

"I know," Rayna says, "and I'm not mad at you.

You don't have to believe. I do. If Nico did move on, he moved on somewhere better, where I can meet him one day and we'll be together again."

I don't know that I buy that. Sounds to me like a tragic waste—a life spent looking forward to something that won't happen until after you die. I don't say that, though. I go on and explain that Sage is mortal now, and I tell her about his new problems: the nausea, the exhaustion, the memory loss. I can't bring myself to tell her about him throwing me into the wall; it's too awful. Finally I tell her about Ben's ominous diagnosis.

"Which is what's happening now," she says. "Madness and violence."

"What do you mean?"

"I don't know Sage that well, but I never pegged him as a crush-your-hands kind of guy. You must be terrified."

"We'll find a way to get him better. I'm sure of it."

"It's okay to be terrified," she says. "It doesn't make you weak or anything. And even if it did, there are worse things than weak."

Tears spring to my eyes. I had no idea I was holding so much in until Rayna sliced right through it. "I missed you so much," I say.

"I missed you, too." Then she yawns, and she laughs when she can barely pry her eyes back open. "Oh my gosh, I think I'm talking in my sleep. I should go back home."

"Don't. Stay over. We'll sleep on the couches." The gray living room couches were always our favorite place for slumber parties, because they're as wide as full-size beds but even cushier, and they offer the added bonus of letting us fall asleep to bad TV. I loan Rayna something to sleep in, and I check on Sage before I go downstairs. He's asleep in the spare room. I make sure the house alarm is set before Rayna and I go to bed. I might not need to keep Sage a secret from Rayna anymore, but I don't want him to slip out and wander again.

I don't have to worry. Rayna and I wake up long before Sage. By the time he comes down, she and I are in the kitchen, and Rayna's scrounging deep in the pantry for something to eat. With a smolderingly sexy smile, Sage covers the distance to me in a heartbeat and gives me a kiss I feel in my toes. I push him away, very gently. I give him a meaningful stare, then glance toward Rayna.

She's frozen at the door to the pantry, and looks like she's going to throw up.

Sage clears his throat uncomfortably and steps

away from me. "Oh, um . . . Rayna. I . . ." He blows through his lips and leans heavily on the counter, completely at a loss. "Clea?"

"She knows. She saw you last night."

"No, she didn't."

I glance at Rayna, who raises an eyebrow.

"She did," I say. "She walked in on us, and—"

Sage's laugh is dry and mirthless. "Don't lie to me, Clea. I think I'd remember something like that."

"It's okay. You forgot. You forget things sometimes. It's not a big deal."

"You're *lying*!" he yells, slapping his hands on the island and leaning into my face. "I don't 'forget things.' I'm perfectly fine."

Every muscle in his body is tensed, and his jaw pulses in and out. He's on the edge, and I have to tread carefully.

"Of course you're fine. I never said you weren't."

"You're trying to turn her against me, aren't you? You want to turn everyone against me."

"What? No."

"She's not," Rayna pipes up. "She hasn't said anything bad about you."

"Stay out of this!" he roars, wheeling on Rayna, who pales.

"Please don't yell at her. I promise, everything's okay." I reach out for him, hoping the contact will center him, but he just sneers at our stacked hands like they're a dead bug, then slides his hand away and stalks back upstairs. "You don't know anything," he mutters as he goes.

Rayna and I stare at the spot where he had been.

"So that was pleasant," she says.

"It's new. He used to understand that he had memory problems. Even if he didn't know what happened, he understood something had."

"So he's getting worse?"

I don't want to answer. I don't have to.

"I'm going to go talk to him," I say.

I find Sage in my room, staring at the picture of himself he drew. I taped it to the wall before Rayna and I went to bed last night. I wish I could see into his head. Is he feeling frightened? Sad for what he lost? Angry? Hopeless?

I love Sage. I know he's the only man for me, and that I'm meant to be with him forever . . . but sometimes I also feel like I know nothing about him.

Slowly, I reach up to rest my hand on his shoulder. "Are you okay?"

"Did I really see Rayna last night?"

"You did."

His back hunches a little. "I'm sorry I got so angry. I can't explain it. I was furious, like I wanted to . . ." He can't say it, but I'm afraid I know what he means.

"We'll get you through this," I promise him. "You'll be okay."

Sage doesn't answer, but he turns around and lets me hold him. He's so big and strong, but I'm the one supporting him.

I hope I'm strong enough to handle it.

eight

CLEA

An hour later Sage is back to himself, hanging out with Rayna and me in the living room. Rayna sits opposite him, leaning forward as she pelts him with questions.

"Where are you from?"

"Originally? Italy. But I don't remember anything about it."

"How many brothers and sisters do you have?"

"I don't have any."

We're a good half hour into the prosecution. While I was upstairs with Sage, Rayna had a brainstorm. She thought Sage's real problem might be that Nico's soul is still inside him, fighting to win back his body. She started grilling Sage with rapid-fire questions to see if any of his answers were anything Nico would say.

"The scar on your left hip: What kind of animal is it shaped like?"

Sage frowns, then pulls down his waistband and twists to look.

"Hey, look at that," he laughs. "It's an otter!"

"It's not an otter," Rayna says. "It's a prairie dog. Otters have tails."

"Really?" Sage says. "I think it looks like an otter."

"I thought it was more of a cat," I say. Then Rayna glares at me. "Sorry."

She studies Sage with a squinty-eyed glare. "I'm not convinced. I still think you're in a turf war with Nico."

"It's impossible," I say. "The only way the soul transfer could work was if Nico's body was empty."

"I guess . . ."

"So we're back to where we were."

We sit with that for a moment, then hear the long beep as the front door opens. Ben has the alarm code, and he taps it in the keypad to stop the shrill warning wail.

"Hey, guys," he says as he pops his head in the room. "I found something I think will help—"

That's when he sees Rayna on the other couch. She waggles her fingers at him. Ben splutters on his coffee. "Oh. Hey. Um—You— He— It—"

"Any other pronouns you want to throw in there?" Rayna asks.

Ben plops down on the couch next to her but is still at a loss for words.

"I came over last night," Rayna says. "I know everything."

"Everything?" Ben croaks.

She takes his hand and squeezes it. "I don't blame you. It's not your fault he's gone."

Tears well in Ben's eyes, and when he tries to speak, nothing comes out but a sob. He runs his hands over his face and tries again. "I didn't mean it to happen. I just wanted to push him away from Sage, and then . . . and then . . ."

He cries outright then, and she pulls him toward her so he can sob in her arms. It's like one of Wanda's mother-bear hugs, but with all that oversize comfort and power squeezed into Rayna's small body. She rubs Ben's back and makes shushing noises until he sits up again. He's a little sniffly, a little splotchy-faced, but better.

"You said you found something out?" I ask.

Ben takes a deep breath to collect himself. "Yeah. So I've been checking out ancient texts at the library, and I realized a lot of the material on soul-switching reminded me of Walk-Ins."

"Walk-Ins?"

"Yes. It's a phenomenon where one soul leaves a body, and another . . . *walks in*."

"Like . . ." I nod to Sage, but Ben grimaces.

"Only sort of," he says. "Usually a Walk-In is a lot less . . . violent. And it's done more by choice. A higher-plane agreement between two souls. The living one is tired and wants to move on; the other soul wants to come back to the bodily world."

"So they just . . . switch?" Rayna asks.

Ben nods. "It's usually pretty seamless. The body goes to sleep, then wakes up with a brand-new soul. But sometimes it's a little more challenging. A soul that wants to leave a body might have a hard time letting go, or one that wants to come in might get stuck along the way. When that happens, there are ceremonies and rituals that can help."

I notice Sage getting agitated next to me. His knee jounces up and down, and his hands flex in and out of fists.

"We don't need a soul-switching ceremony," I say. "We're there already."

"Hear me out," Ben says. "The whole Walk-In angle led me from the old books to periodicals— New Agey magazines that are ninety-eight percent garbage, but there's still that two percent real stuff. I found an article about a commune in Sedona that's all about Walk-Ins."

"Ohhhh," Rayna nods. "Sedona's *very* spiritual. It's built at the convergence point of several spiritual vortexes. Yoga in Sedona is life-changing."

Ben tilts his head dubiously. "So they say. Anyway, wannabe Walk-Ins come to this commune when they're ready to make the switch. Sometimes they go alone, sometimes with their friends or family members or other believers who want to help them through, and the leader of the place facilitates the swap and makes sure everything goes okay."

"Do you think it's legitimate?" I ask.

"Don't know. Honestly, the fact that it's in Sedona makes me more leery. That's where you put a place when you want to attract wanna-believers.

No offense," he adds to Rayna. She shrugs it off.

"But if it's real . . . if it's even a little real . . . then this is a place that deals with soul transfers all the time. With that kind of volume, it's likely they'd also have experience with soul rejection, and maybe know what to do about it."

Sage's agitation is growing. Both knees are bouncing now, and his eyes shift around the room like he's looking to escape.

"So let's contact them and ask," I say.

"That's the thing," Ben says. "They never gave the name of the place in the article, and they didn't say exactly where it is or how to contact them. Apparently they've had trouble from myth-buster types, so they like to keep everything pretty secret. I was going to go through your dad's studio today and see if he had any information."

"Oh!" Rayna pipes up. "Maybe Alissa Grande can help!"

I grin. Alissa Grande's the name I use as a professional photojournalist. "It's true," I say. "The magazine world's pretty small. If you show me the article, it might take a while, but I could probably track down the writer and pick his brain."

Sage loudly pushes the coffee table out of his way as he jumps up and stalks out of the room, pounding the jamb on the way out. His footsteps echo as he stomps out the front door and slams it behind him. Ben and Rayna both look at me for advice, but I just shrug.

"I moved the car keys; he won't go far."

I don't like the idea of Sage storming around in his current state, but I've learned that chasing him won't help. I'll do more for him by staying here with Ben and Rayna and trying to find out more about the Walk-In place.

"Here's a printout of the article," Ben says, pulling the pages out of his notebook. "I'm going to head downstairs."

He does, and Rayna slips to her house to grab her laptop, then brings it up to my room so she can do Walk-In research while I make calls and send e-mails to try and track down the writer of the article. Every time I hang up the phone, she pipes up with something she's reading.

"Clea . . . two souls *can* share a body."

"What do you mean?"

"That's how some of these Walk-Ins start. The second soul moves in and hangs with the first one in the same body."

"Like a roommate?"

"*Exactly* like a roommate. But a temporary

roommate, just until they figure out who's staying and who's leaving. Then the original soul moves out and the first one takes over."

"So more like a sublet than a roommate situation."

"Except the subletter never gives the apartment back. I can't find any stories where the original soul comes back once it's left. The ones that do aren't really Walk-Ins, they're more like demonic possessions.

"NO WAY!" Rayna screams while I'm in the middle of another call. I walk out to finish, and when I come back in, she's standing on top of my bed, staring at her laptop screen.

"Rayna?"

"'While many Walk-Ins exhibit physical changes such as a shift in posture or tone of voice,'" Rayna launches in, reading without preamble, "'Deirdre Kelley's friends knew something drastic had happened to the woman because *even the color of her eyes had changed*'!"

She lowers the computer and gapes at me, waiting for my response. I'm nowhere near as gobsmacked as she is, but she's obviously expecting something huge from me, and I don't want to bring her down. "That's . . . amazing. But we're not looking for proof that Sage is in Nico's body. We already know that."

"Yes! We know the Sage/Nico thing is real, but if the Walk-Ins have the same symptoms—especially something as big as eye color changing—they're probably real too!"

"Hopefully the ones at the place in Sedona are real," I say as my phone rings. I check the caller ID. "Randolph Greene. It's the guy who wrote the article!" I tell Rayna.

She bounces off the bed and runs to my side as I answer, then go ahead and put him on speakerphone. If Greene notices, he doesn't say. And I get the feeling he *would* say. For a man whose credits all have titles like *The Guiding Path of Serenity* and *Living Calmly in the Now*, he's very blunt and abrupt. His voice has a nicotine rasp, and he barks out every sentence like he's training marines.

"The Walk-Ins?" he asks when I bring up the article. "They're nuts!"

"Really? Because your article seemed very positive about the phenomenon. . . ."

"'Cause I wanted to get paid!" Then he checks himself, adding a layer of velvety smoothness to his words. "Unless of course you're affiliated with the group. Lovely people, they are. Just lovely."

Rayna covers her mouth as she snorts.

"No," I say. "I'm not."

"So you're not a freak. Good. Miranda vouched for you, but you never know. What do you need?"

I tell him I'm researching an article and would love the name and location of the Walk-Ins' commune. I promise him I won't let anyone know where I got it.

"Don't. They're crazy. Especially Burnham Brightley. That one's crazy-brilliant."

"Burnham Brightley?"

"He runs the place. 'Transitions,' he calls it. Charges an arm and a leg for people to go and ease their way from one inner soul to another. He knew I was doing a puff piece, but he still wouldn't let me go anywhere without him, and he wouldn't let me ask any questions. Residents came and told me their stories, that's all I got."

"Interesting. So what do you think would be the best way to approach him for an interview?"

Greene laughs. "Good luck. After my piece he had some lawsuit against him, trying to pin him as a fraud, asking for all kinds of damages. No clue what happened with it, but I hear he's even more clamped down than before. Don't blame him; place has to be a cash cow. Last thing he wants is an exposé that'll keep the loons away."

We talk a little more, and after I assure him again that his name will stay out of things, he tells me Transitions' address and phone number.

"So it's a total scam?" Rayna says when I hang up.

"Greene thinks so. At least, he thinks Brightley's a fake . . . but that doesn't mean everyone who *goes* to Transitions is a fake."

"He just thinks they're crazy."

"And all those who'd be called crazy if they told everyone the true story of the last six months?" I ask. Rayna smiles as we both lift our hands. "Brightley may or may not have real information. But remember in the article it said some people stick around after they transitioned to help other people? If even a few of those are genuine Walk-Ins, they're immersed in that world. They could have information that would help Sage."

"Maybe."

"Unless it's different with a Walk-In because the new soul was invited in," I say, "so maybe the body's less likely to reject it."

"Body and soul are two different things. Just because the soul agrees to the swap, the body might not be on board." Rayna draws a deep breath, then says, "Clea, what if that's happening with Nico? What if his body doesn't want Sage to be there?"

"It's possible, I guess. Whatever the reason, Sage is getting worse, and I feel like the people at Transitions are the first real chance we have to get help."

"I think so too. But do you really think they'll talk to us on the phone?"

"No, I don't. If we want to talk to the Walk-Ins, we need to go in with one."

nine

"You should have told me," Ben says. "That was *exactly* the kind of thing you were supposed to write down in the notebook."

The rows in the plane are so close together that all he has to do is lean forward a little and his voice is right in my ear. Sage and I are in one row of two, me on the aisle, with Ben right behind me and Rayna right behind Sage. Sage is asleep, or Ben and I wouldn't be having this conversation.

"I know," I say, "but I was handling it."

We've been going over this again and again since

last night. Once I'd decided on our new plan, I went to find Sage and tell him. That left Rayna and Ben in the house together, and she told him about Sage's violent episodes. He cornered me later and I admitted everything to him, and while he's been smart enough not to say anything in front of Sage, he hisses my ear off about it every chance he gets.

"Handling it? You got your head busted open. You still don't know what the hell he did before you found him in Rhode Island. He could have assaulted someone."

"I'm sure he didn't assault anyone."

"*How* are you sure?"

I'm not sure at all. The truth is, I've been torturing myself about it for days, scouring the papers online and holding my breath while I wait for a story about a random body left in the woods. But I don't want to say that to Ben.

"He'd have wanted you to tell me," Ben says. "If he was in his right mind, you know he would. He told us what he wanted me to do."

I wheel in my seat to face him. "He doesn't need to be locked up. Look at where we are. We're taking steps to heal him. And you're here, right? That should make you feel better."

My original plan hadn't involved Ben coming to Sedona. I wanted him and Rayna to stay with Sage and keep an eye on him while I went alone. When Sage refused to stick around without me, Rayna insisted on coming too, to help me handle him, which Ben thought was a joke. If Sage acted out at Transitions, I'd need more than just Rayna's help. Much as I hated to admit it, he was right, so now there's four of us jetting out to Arizona.

Sage groans in his sleep and shifts mightily. His knees push against the seat in front of him, and the woman sitting there glares back at us. I give her an apologetic, close-lipped smile and wish I'd thought to upgrade us to business class. Ben, meanwhile, leans back in his seat, and I'm grateful for the break in his diatribe.

After a five-hour flight and a two-hour drive, we get to Sedona. The minute we cross the town line, it's like the atmosphere gets thinner and we can all breathe again. It's so beautiful, like driving through a watercolor. Giant red striated rocks burst out of the ground on either side of the road, standing in stark contrast to the crystal-blue sky. Even the roadside scrub seems green, lush, and — okay, fine — energized. As if on cue, all four of us roll down our windows. I'm in the back with Rayna, and I take a deep breath to drink in the desert air. It works its way through my body and makes me feel loose and calm. Sage and Ben are feeling it too, I can tell. In the passenger seat, Sage closes his eyes against the soothing wind, then reaches his hands back and presses his palms against the roof of the car, stretching himself long. Ben rests his elbow on the window and bounces his head to music only he can hear.

Maybe there's something to healing vibrations after all.

The plan is to go right to Transitions. We have an appointment. I called yesterday from my cell, which has caller ID blocked. I told the receptionist I was "Clementine," that "my sister, Charlotte" was weary of the world, had already reached an agreement with a spirit now sharing her body, and needed help transitioning to the beyond. At that point I knew we'd all be going, so I said Charlotte would be accompanied by me, our brother (actually Sage), and my husband (Ben). When I told the receptionist we'd be flying in the next day, she took down our flight time and said she'd be happy to welcome us the minute we landed.

We rented a car with GPS, so we wouldn't get lost. It's good we did, because the place is almost impossible to find. There's no sign, and the entrance all but disappears among the succulents. Even after we turn and pass the twin stone walls that flank the driveway, we can only assume we're in the right spot.

"Smile," I say. "If they're as careful here as Randolph Greene said, I'm sure we're already on camera."

The driveway winds over half a mile of desert, and when we eventually see the building, it looks like nothing special—a flat, square adobe in a sandy color that blends in with the grounds.

"Okay," I say, "let's go over it one last time. I'm Charlotte." I turn to Rayna. "You're Clementine, and you called yesterday and spoke to the receptionist. Ben, you're my brother-in-law—"

"Does that mean he's married to me?" Rayna asks.

"Yeah."

"Ew."

"What?" Ben says. "Like that would be so horrible?"

"Not horrible, just . . . weird. Can we maybe be separated?"

"Get over it," I say. "It's a pretend marriage. Sage . . ."

Sage is agitated again, his jaw working as he taps his fingers in an unsteady rhythm on the roof of the car. His episodes come fast and furious now. I'm amazed he hasn't had one since we left, but there's only so long our luck can hold out.

Apparently he knows what I'm thinking. He turns and gives me a smile. "I'm here. I'm good."

I want to believe him, but there's a sheen of sweat on his face, and I don't think it's from the desert air. Still, I know better than to challenge him.

"Great," I say. "So you're all believers, and you're all checking in to be with me while I transition."

Ben pulls into a parking spot, and I only start to panic as we get out of the car.

What am I doing? I take pictures, I'm no undercover reporter. I don't do sting operations, or embed myself with military groups. And it's not like I can act. What makes me think I can pull this off?

Sage squeezes my hand as he helps me out, then leans close and whispers in my ear, "You don't have to do this. We'll find another way."

He says it . . . but I know it's not true. We've looked for another way and haven't found anything yet. If we had more time, maybe this wouldn't be our first choice, but Sage's soul is losing its grip. He needs answers, and this is the best chance we have of finding them.

Besides, I remind myself, I really have nothing to be afraid of. Burnham Brightley might do anything to protect his moneymaking scheme, but it's not like I'm out to expose it. He can bilk as many gullible people out of their money as he wants, as far as I'm concerned. The information I need has nothing to do with all that.

We walk in a close knot as we make our way toward the entrance. Sedona might have a warm and healing energy, but Transitions does not, and we all feel it. There's something ominous about the place. The door is as brown as the rest of the building. There's no welcome mat, no sign, no knocker or doorbell. There isn't even a door*knob*.

Ben knocks, but no one answers. It's Rayna who finds the intercom on the wall to the right. It's the same dirt brown that blends into every other surface we can see. If I was really a Walk-In about to spend my life's savings on an extended stay, I'd be seriously bummed out.

"Hello?" comes a voice through the intercom.

"Hi," Rayna says. "It's me, Clementine. I spoke to you on the phone yesterday about my sister, Charlotte?"

"Oh, yes!" the voice says. "We're all ready for you. Come in."

We hear a buzz, and Ben pushes on the door. It gives easily, and we move inside from a world of beige and brown to full Technicolor. When the door closes behind us, it's almost impossible to believe this lush wonderland was even attached to what we saw up front. The lobby has no back wall—it's open to the grounds and the red rock mountains in the distance, a color echoed in the red terra-cotta tiles on the floor. These end at a lush green lawn that spreads around a black-bottomed amoeba-shaped pool, with a raised circular Jacuzzi at one end. A waterfall flows from the Jacuzzi to the pool, and while I know it's manufactured, it looks like a completely natural oasis. Giant flowers add bursts of red, yellow, orange, and pink to the landscape.

We're clearly all staring, because the receptionist clucks her understanding. "You'd never know it from the outside, right? Spirit Burnham did it that way on purpose. He built into a hillside so we'd have more privacy." The woman is tiny, and looks almost exactly like a sunflower. An older sunflower that's starting to wither, but a sunflower nonetheless. She wears a green pantsuit and has a leathery, suntanned face and a mane of frizzy blond hair. When she gestures outside, I see that both her hands are folded in on themselves, curled by severe arthritis. "I'm Spirit Bitsy. You just enjoy the view. I'll go get Spirit Burnham."

She clicks across the tile on four-inch heels that mean she's even shorter than I imagined. I don't know what's more remarkable, her tiny stature or that at her age she can still walk on stilettos.

"The minute we check in, I'm jumping in that pool," Rayna says.

"*Clementine...* ," I say, trying to remind her we're surely on camera and won't be welcomed if they think we're crashing.

"Right. Sorry, Charlotte."

I look up at Sage and follow his gaze to the chairs on the lawn. Two heavyset men play cards, while a young woman relaxes on a chaise. Is he wondering if one of them knows how to save him from soul rejection? I am. The place gives me more creeps than warm fuzzies, but something tells me we're in the right spot to get answers.

"Good afternoon, my friends!" Burnham Brightley coos. The man is almost disturbingly well tanned, and when he shakes, he does so with a double-handed grip. He wears a crisp white suit, his posture is perfect, and he exudes power, charisma, and a friendliness that makes you want to lean toward him and get closer. If it weren't for the jarring slight surfer-boy accent and the fashion-crime Birkenstocks on his feet, I'd mistake him for Mr. Roarke on *Fantasy Island*.

He shakes my hand last, and cradles it in his while he looks deep into my eyes. "Spirit Charlotte, it is an honor that you've chosen our little slice of paradise in which to make your transition. We do not take your trust lightly, and I promise you we'll make this fork in the road as seamless and beautiful as possible."

He's good. I almost wish I *was* transitioning; he makes it sound so lovely. "Thank you."

"Now just take a moment to say your goodbyes and we'll get you checked in."

Good-byes?

"Wait," I splutter. "I thought friends and family could stay and be involved in the process."

"That used to be the case, yes," Brightley says, "but we've since changed our policy. Unfortunately, we've had some bad experiences with supporting guests who came in with the wrong energy and threatened to sabotage everything we work to achieve. While I'm sure none of you would do such a thing, the stakes are just too high for our transitioners. It's not a risk we can take. I'm sure you understand."

I understand that whatever lawsuits Brightley faced have made him gun-shy. He only wants the true believers. My throat constricts when I think of staying here by myself, and I try to talk him out of it. "I'm sorry, but my sister told your receptionist we'd all be coming. I heard her."

"And they're welcome to be here, Charlotte. To drop you off, not to stay. If Spirit Bitsy gave you another impression, I apologize. So please say your good-byes, then we can quickly handle all the nagging bookkeeping and paperwork and get you settled in your new home."

Sage puts his hands firmly on my shoulders. I

lean back slightly, letting his strength prop me up. "One question first," Sage asks, "how many other residents do you have here now?"

I immediately recognize what he's doing. He wants to make sure there are enough people around that it's worth the risk of me being here alone.

"At the moment we have ten transitioners, plus five facilitators who have already transitioned and choose to stay on and help others. It's an option we offer, for those who don't wish to go back into the outside world. There's a fee, of course, but the calling comes with great satisfaction." Brightley turns to me, his eyes brimming with ersatz kindness. "You might choose that route yourself."

Ten transitioners and five facilitators. That's fifteen people who might know something that can help. We only need one.

"That sounds nice," I say meekly. My plan is to say pretty much everything meekly as Charlotte, since I'm supposed to be the soul who wants out. Fifteen people shouldn't take that long to interview, either. A few days, tops.

Sage gives voice to my thoughts. "Clementine

never found out the length of stay," he says. "If we can't be here with Charlotte, when can we get her? When can we see her?"

"You won't see Spirit Charlotte at all, now will you? You'll see . . ."

He turns to me for a response.

"Spirit Krysta," I supply.

He smiles warmly. "Spirit Krysta, then. That's who you'll see. When she has arrived and is ready."

"Assuming she wants to see *you*," Spirit Bitsy giggles. "After all, she's a whole new person. You never know!"

"Thank you, Spirit Bitsy," Brightley says tightly, and Bitsy immediately clams up and looks at the floor. "As for visiting hours," he continues, "they're entirely dependent on how Spirit Charlotte is feeling. If you provide Spirit Bitsy with all your numbers, she'll be sure to call and let you know."

On cue, Spirit Bitsy grabs a clipboard and passes it around to Rayna, Sage, and Ben so they can write down their numbers.

"Very well," Brightley says. "Now, Spirit Charlotte . . . are we ready?"

I feel Sage's hands tighten on my shoulders.

I reach up and cover them with mine, but it's Brightley's eyes that I meet.

"Spirit Charlotte and Spirit Krysta are both ready," I say.

Brightley nods, and I turn to my family. My fake family, but they're as much my real family as anyone. The three of them all look frightened for me, but there's no reason. It's just that we weren't expecting to split up, and now we are. And sure, this place is a little creepy, especially since I'm pretty sure Brightley's just a con man trying to wheedle money out of people, but when I'm ready to leave, I can say that "Spirit Krysta" has arrived and taken over, then I'll check out . . . ideally with a way to help heal Sage.

Easy.

I hug Ben and Rayna first, then Sage, gripping on to him as tightly as I can. I lift onto tiptoes and kiss him on the cheek in as sisterly a way as I can manage, then bring my lips to his ear to whisper, "You'll hear from me within twenty-four hours. I love you."

"Off we go then!" Spirit Bitsy says, and shoos them out the door. Sage's eyes gazing back at me are the last thing I see before it slams shut.

That's when I notice there's no knob on this side of the door either.

"Well then," Brightley says, draping an arm over my shoulder. "Let's get you situated, Spirit Charlotte. Shall we?"

ten

"Okay, let's just say it out loud, 'cause the silence is killing me: It totally sucks leaving Clea there."

I'm in the backseat of the car, sitting willingly in the bitch seat because it's easier that way to lean forward and talk to Ben and Sage.

Not that we've been talking. Ben grips the steering wheel like he's going to choke the thing, and Sage stares out the window doing that weirdo thing with his jaw muscle that makes his cheek throb in and out. He's super sullen, with his eyebrows pulled low over his eyes and his shoulders tense and hunched.

Not that there's anything wrong with being upset, given the situation. I just mention it because it's so not in any way how Nico would ever look, even if he was as worried as Sage is right now.

That's the crazy thing. To me, Sage doesn't even look like Nico anymore. At all. I mean, I know Sage is in Nico's body and in fact looks *exactly* like Nico, but honestly, I don't see it. It's amazing how much the soul inside affects a body. It makes me want to become friends with a bunch of identical twins so I can see if the same thing's true with them.

As much as I can't see Nico in that body anymore, I keep wondering . . . Is there any of him there? Clea doesn't seem to think so, so I let it drop with her, but I can't help but think Sage would have an easier time in the body if Nico was okay with having him there. And doesn't part of him have to *be* there in order to not be okay with it? And if part of him is there . . . shouldn't he get to control his own body and not Sage?

I don't want to think about it . . . but I think about it constantly.

"We need a place to stay," Ben says. "I don't

have anything booked; we thought we'd all be at Transitions."

"We never should have left her there," Sage says.

"What were you going to do, go caveman and sling her over your shoulder?" I ask.

"I just don't like it."

"Of course you don't. It would be creepy if you liked it. None of us like it. But honestly? The three of you have been chased by guys with guns and knives. You've had trees thrown at you. I'm pretty sure Clea can handle being on lockdown with some crazy people. And if it means she can find something out that'll save your life, that's what she'd choose to do."

Sage doesn't say anything for a while, just looks grimly out the window. Then he says, "We should stay close. We want to get there right away when 'Spirit Bitsy' calls."

"Spirit Bitsy," Ben snarks under his breath, and a second later we're all laughing, even Sage. Then we're all talking over one another about everything we saw until Sage cries out, "There!"

It's good that he was looking out the window, because the little white colonial-style building with the shutters and balconies looks way more like someone's private home than a bed-and-breakfast. If Sage hadn't seen the small sign in front, we'd never have known it was the Presswood Inn. They have vacancies, and we get two rooms that share an adjoining bathroom. This sounds like a serious issue for me until I see the deep tub, complete with bubble bath, water pillow, and TV mounted for the best possible lounge-and-watch angle. I sincerely hope the guys aren't planning to use the room, because it is my goal to be soaking in there until we get the call to visit Clea.

Mitch and Molly, bar-none the cutest innkeepers in the universe, give us the scoop on everything there is to do in Sedona, which is pretty mind-blowing. Hikes and bike paths and horse trails so beautiful that even I would cave and go aerobic. They also know all about the energy vortexes, and recommend yoga groups I'd love. When all this is over, Clea and I have to come back and take advantage of it all. Right now none of us want to leave the Presswood. It'll be faster to get to Clea if we're all in the same place, as close as possible to Transitions.

While the deep tub is beyond enticing, I decide to save it for the evening and spend the entire afternoon in the outdoor pool, with its impossible views of Bell Rock and Courthouse Rock . . . which kind of look like a bell and a courthouse. At least, that's what Molly tells me when she comes by with homemade lemonade she lets me drink as I lounge on a floaty in the water.

It's the perfect place to wait for Clea, who I'm sure will be fine. She'll talk to some people, get some information, then leave. And if it takes her a couple of days to do it, I'm willing to sacrifice that time when I should be at school and instead spend it here. In the pool. Staring at giant red rocks. Sipping homemade lemonade.

I look into the bay window that juts onto the lawn surrounding the pool, and I see Ben and Sage bent over something. A card game, probably. Molly and Mitch showed us their whole stash of games, and when they pulled out the cribbage board, I could see Ben's fingers start twitching like an Old West villain before a shootout.

I don't get the card thing. Much better to be outside in the water. I swim a few laps to stretch my muscles, then climb back onto the floaty and contemplate the massive rocks jutting out of the earth. The more I look at them, the more I feel their magical energy, and I know I can help Clea even from here. I meditate on her success, sending positive energy across the desert. I feel it streaming out of me, flowing to her, giving her strength. Then, when I see her in my mind's eye filled with energy head to toe, I meditate on Nico—his *soul*, not his body.

I sink deeper into relaxation and concentrate on sending my energy to him. I want to reach out across the divide between here and beyond. I need to know if he's there—safe, happy, and cared for. Not here, worried about the fate of his body. I need to know he's in a better place. And if for some reason he's having trouble getting there or getting used to it, if he's worried about me or his family or anything he left behind, I need him to know he can relax. We're all okay down here, and while I might not have his soul here with me, I still love him, and we'll be together again one day, in what to him will feel like a blink.

I concentrate hard on all that. I try to feel Nico's spirit and energy and get peace in the knowledge that he's out there and okay . . . but I can't do it. Probably that's because my meditation skills aren't that great. I can do yoga all day and night, but sinking into myself to get out of myself has never been my strongest point. I'd just hoped that with the help of Sedona and those unbelievable rocks I could do it.

Maybe if I try harder.

I stay in the pool until sunset, but I don't get any vibe from Nico's spirit. I've barely moved in hours, but I'm exhausted from all the meditating. Isn't meditating supposed to leave you energized? Maybe I'm doing it wrong.

I shouldn't be so disappointed. It's not like it's easy to sink into a state of pure spirit so strong you can feel souls that have moved on. But Nico's my soulmate. I thought I could reach him. It would feel so good. Now I have to wonder: Did I fail because I'm not good enough at meditating, or because Nico's soul is stuck somewhere and can't be reached?

"Rayna, sweetie?" Molly calls from the edge of the pool. "It's dinnertime."

"You serve dinner? I thought it was just breakfast."

"Breakfast is included, but we offer dinner, too, and the boys said you'd rather stay in tonight."

The boys. I giggle to myself. Like we're her kids.

I climb out of the pool and head inside, where the aromas from the kitchen make my stomach scream in anticipation. I take the fastest shower in the world and zip down to the dining room, where Mitch and "the boys" are already tucking into a salad with sun-dried tomatoes and olives and parmesan and . . . I'm drooling.

"Who won?" I ask as I sit next to Mitch, across from Sage and Ben, and Molly instantly swings out of the kitchen with my own plate of the salad. I attack it. Delicious.

Ben shoots me a warning glare.

"You're saying you lost?"

He shakes his head slightly, and I look at Sage, who's stabbing his salad like it insulted him. I can hear the fork tines pinging off the plate. So can Mitch and Molly. They look concerned—twin worry lines crease their foreheads. I feel bad for them.

"Sage, the lettuce is already dead. Maybe you should go easy on it."

Sage stabs his fork into the middle of the plate and lifts his face just enough to sneer at me. "Maybe you should shut your mouth."

I want to rip his tongue out.

I know Sage's soul is struggling to keep its place in Nico's body, but it disgusts me. Nico would never talk to me that way, and he'd roll over in his grave if he knew what his body was doing. To me it's blasphemy.

"Who wants fresh-baked rolls?" Molly asks, leaping up from her chair.

"I told Mitch and Molly that Sage isn't feeling so well after our trip," Ben says pointedly. "In fact, I thought he might be better off taking dinner in our room."

"Want to stop talking about me like I'm not here?" Sage growls.

Stop it! I scream inside my head. *You're abusing him! You're abusing his body!*

"Mitch, the pool is soooo relaxing," I say, eager to change Mitch's drop-jawed expression. I get the sense that he and mild-mannered Molly have never seen anyone act this rude in their inn before, and they don't know how to deal.

"Why, thank you, Rayna," Mitch says, his cherubic face happy once more. "I can tell you I've spent many an hour getting away from it all in that very spot."

I'm not sure what the "all" is he has to "get away from," but I'm glad he looks happy again. Sage, however, is fuming. His face has turned from pale to crimson, and I wouldn't be surprised to see smoke and ash pour out of his ears.

"I have an idea!" I say. "Mitch, let's go out to the pool right now!"

"Don't you think I know what you're doing?" Sage explodes. He pounds his hands on the table and leans so far over, he almost vaults to our side. Mitch recoils so quickly he knocks over his glass of wine, which spreads a bloodred stain over their white linen tablecloth just as Molly bustles in, cooing about "piping-hot rolls!" She gasps at the sight of Sage looming over her husband and drops the ceramic bread bowl, which crashes into bits. Sage doesn't notice any of it.

"Who are you, and what do you want from me?" he screams in Mitch's face.

"What? I—I'm sure I don't . . ."

Mitch does his best to shrink into his chair, and I can't take it anymore. I jump up and get right in Sage's face. "Stop it! You can't do this to him!"

I feel Mitch's and Molly's faces turn to me, and I feel horrible that they think I'm crazy now too, but I can't let Sage abuse Nico this way.

Sage reaches across the table and grabs my cheeks in his hand so hard I think my jaw will break. He pulls my face close, tugging me until my feet leave the floor. "You want to get in my way?" he asks. "You want to hurt me? I won't let you hurt me."

Ben yells at Sage to stop, but he only squeezes

tighter, until I'm sure my face will crack. Then Molly takes one of the piping-hot rolls and jams it in Sage's eye. He howls and releases the pressure on my face just enough for me to slip out of his grip. He takes two steps back from the table, panting and seething like a wild animal. Ben catches my eye, but before we can do anything Sage grabs a carving knife off the table and throws it down so hard it sticks point-first in the table. Molly screams, Mitch goes deathly pale, and Sage races upstairs. We all jump at the gunshot sound of his door slamming shut.

The two innkeepers exchange a look.

"Maybe the three of you should check out a little early," Molly says.

She does end up changing her mind, though it takes several hours and monumental amounts of charm from Ben and me. We explain that Sage just went through a terrible breakup and he's really not himself, which leads to all of us sharing breakup stories, a lot of laughing, then hours of charades, all of which seem to make everything okay.

That, and the fact that we agree to replace the dining room table.

After Mitch and Molly go to bed, Ben and I

sit across from each other in the giant padded bay window seat. The moon is full, lighting up the majestic red rocks just beyond the inn. I gaze out at them, wishing they'd bring me peace, but I can't find it.

"I hate what he's doing to Nico's body," I say. "It isn't right."

"No," Ben says. "It's not."

The moonlight is good to Ben. He's always bragging about his new workout routine and how buff he's getting, and I love giving him a hard time about it, but the truth is he looks great. Not bulky, just lean and strong. I can see the slight outline of his pecs under his T-shirt, and the shadows cast by the muscles in his arms. Even his face looks different, a little stronger and tougher. Or maybe that's just the late-night scruff on his jaw and chin. I never saw it in him before, but he looks like someone you could lean on.

"We told Molly and Mitch that Sage isn't dangerous," I say. "Did we lie?"

Ben runs one hand through his hair. "I don't know. How does your jaw feel?"

I run my hand over the tender skin. "Like we lied."

Ben nods. "He's getting worse. Paranoid. It's

all part of the same thing. His body's rejecting his soul, so everything's getting detached and confused."

"Hopefully Clea will figure out how to fix it."

"Yeah," he agrees, but he looks distracted.

"What are you thinking about?"

"I just wonder . . ." He scrunches his mouth and shakes his head. "No, I shouldn't say."

I kick at his shin with my bare foot. "Yeah, that'll make me let it go. Spill."

Ben smiles, but it doesn't reach his eyes. "I don't want to get you upset."

It feels chillier in the room, and I pull up my knees and wrap my arms around them. "It's too late for that, don't you think?"

"Yeah, I guess it is." He sighs. "I just wonder . . . if it's only Nico's *body* that's fighting with Sage's soul."

Now it really is colder in the room. I expect to see my breath when I speak. "I've been wondering the same thing."

"It's possible."

"Is it? Clea said the soul transfer never would have happened unless Nico was gone."

"She's right. And yet . . ." He trails off for so long I can't bear it.

"And yet *what*?"

"Nico's gone. I saw it. I . . ."

His voice catches, and this time when he drifts off I know what he's thinking. I can't even imagine what it must feel like to know you're responsible for someone dying, even if you didn't mean it. I'm sure he feels guilty every time he looks at me. I put my hand on top of his and wait for him to collect himself.

"I just wonder," he continues when he can, "if maybe some part of his soul is still there, inside his body."

"Trapped?" My heart clenches as I imagine it. Nico's soul caught in his own body, unable to control it because Sage has taken over . . . forced to sit back and watch him destroy everything he stood for . . .

I can't breathe.

"Not his whole soul," Ben says, "more of an echo. In some of the stories I've read about soul rejections, that's how they describe it. The echo of a past soul wreaks havoc because it can't rest if its body is occupied by someone else."

"Can't rest?" I think about today in the pool, and how I tried to reach Nico's soul but couldn't. "So you don't think Nico's soul can move on?"

"I don't know. That's why I didn't want to say

anything. If there is a soul echo stuck inside that body . . ."

"It would be horrible. Nico would never want that."

"I agree. And if what's happening to Sage is Nico's way of fighting for peace . . . maybe we should let him get it."

It takes me a second to understand exactly what he means. "But if we don't do anything . . . isn't that the descent into madness and violence and death?"

"For Sage. But for Nico, maybe it's a journey to peace."

It's like Ben just put an immersion blender into my brain and turned it on high. "Wait—we can't just let Sage get worse and worse. He'll be dangerous. *More* dangerous."

"I know. He knew it too. He told me to kill him if it got to that point."

"He . . . *what?*"

"I said no. Then he told me to have him locked up in a mental institution, but it's not like we're family. I can't just ask some place to lock him up and have them do it. He'd have to ask for it himself, or do something horrible and get arrested, then have a judge send him away."

"So we're supposed to stand by and wait for him to do something so bad he'll get arrested? That doesn't make sense."

"I know."

"We need Clea to find something at Transitions," I say. "Then we can heal Sage right away, before he gets any worse." Even as I say it, something clangs in my head. "But wait—if Nico's soul is fighting because it doesn't want Sage in his body, and we force the body to accept Sage . . . what happens to Nico's soul?"

"It's trapped forever," Ben says. "It never finds rest."

No. It's not right. Nico never hurt anyone. It's not fair that his soul might never move on, or get the chance to be with mine in whatever comes next. When I think about it, the ache is so huge it's impossible to contain, like trying to imagine the entire universe. I feel like I'll explode if I try to fit it inside me.

"You really think that's what would happen?" I ask Ben.

"I do. I think . . . I think maybe the only way Nico can rest is if Sage's soul is expelled from his body."

"But Sage would die," I say breathlessly.

"What kind of life does he have now?" Ben asks. "What kind of life will he have if he *does* get worse, and does something horrible, and spends his mortal life locked away? What kind of life will Clea have, watching Sage come completely unglued? That's assuming she survives. He already tried to hurt her. And you. What if he kills someone? I don't think I could live with myself, could you?"

"We have to stop him," I say. "And the only way to do that is heal him . . . even if that sacrifices Nico's soul."

Saying the words nearly kills me, but I don't know if there's another way.

"*Or*," Ben says, "we could stop it by freeing *both* their souls, and letting them both move on."

The circles under Ben's eyes look darker suddenly, and the moonlight casts shadows that sink his cheeks and eyes.

I'm scared, but I'm not sure anymore of what. Maybe of myself and what I'm thinking. I can't let Nico's soul suffer. He doesn't deserve it. And Sage has been alive a very long time. Maybe his soul needs to rest too.

I tremble as I ask, "Do you know how to do that? Expel Sage's soul from Nico's body?"

"Not yet," Ben says, "but from what I've read, I do know there's something I'd need. Something I don't have and maybe you do. Something personal of Nico's. Do you have anything?"

The ring Nico left me weighs heavily against my chest. I pull the heavy gold ring on its chain and hold it in my palm. Ben leans forward, and his head bends close to mine as he studies the swirling loops.

"He left it for me with a note that said, 'One day,'" I say, the words barely more than a whisper.

"It's old. The center is a Celtic triskelion. It represents the unity of spirit, mind, and body. The outside ring surrounding it? That's eternity." Ben looks up from the ring. "Nico was living under a curse. This symbol represented his hope that he'd break it—that his spirit, mind, and body could live forever in unity, free from that curse. He wanted you to have it because he believed 'one day' it would happen . . . and when it did, he wanted his spirit, mind, and body to be with yours, for eternity."

I stare at the ring and imagine Nico's face. Not the way I've seen it lately, warped by Sage's soul, but Nico's own sweet, open smile, and his clear blue eyes. The swirls of the necklace swim as tears fill my eyes, and I squeeze it in my hand before I turn around and lift my hair off my neck.

"Take it," I say, my voice thick in my ears. "Before I change my mind."

Ben unclasps the chain and takes it away. I sob a little as I feel its absence against my chest.

"Find a way to do it." I whisper, my back still turned to Ben. "Free his soul. He deserves that."

Ben doesn't say anything. I feel the heat of his hand above my back, like he wants to comfort me, but I stiffen and he doesn't touch me. I hear his feet as he climbs the stairs.

Alone in the window seat, I stare out at the moon and the red rocks. I focus on Nico's soul and promise him peace.

eleven

CLEA

The first place Burnham Brightley leads me is his office, beautifully decorated but appropriately humble for a man who has dedicated his life to helping others. He's clearly thought of everything. He walks toward a circular mahogany table and pulls out one of the chairs. As I sit on the cushy maroon-upholstered seat, he heads to a sideboard and offers me my choice of refreshments before sitting across from me.

"You're here because you're ready to make a change, yes?"

"Yes," I say in my meek-Charlotte voice.

"You've taken the first step," Brightley says with an oily smile. "Your soul has reached out, and Spirit Krysta answered that call. You must be very grateful to her for that kindness."

He looks so condescending I want to puke. I can only imagine how desperate most of the people who check in here must be if they don't see it.

"I am."

"And yet much as you want to, you and Spirit Krysta are having trouble making the transition."

"Yes," I say, trying to fill my voice with the proper amount of pain and suffering. It's a good thing Charlotte would be a woman of few words; I don't know how much of this I can pull off.

I guess I managed to sound more pained than disgusted, because Brightley frowns sympathetically and places his hand on mine. It feels clammy. "We can help. We will give you the peace you seek, and allow Spirit Krysta to rise in full bloom. However"—he grips my hand with what I think is supposed to be solemn compassion—"we just can't say for sure how long it will take. Some transitions happen almost immediately once the spirits are in our nurturing environment, while other spirits need to be teased out, even if they want to emerge very badly. Does that make sense?"

No. "Of course."

"While you're awaiting transition, you'll be in a very sensitive place, and the last thing we want you thinking about are your finances. That's why we like to take a credit card in advance. We'll charge only the days you use, and we'll return the card at the end of your stay."

I don't have a credit card with Charlotte's name on it, but I have come prepared. I still have Larry Steczynski's black Amex. Larry Steczynski is one of Sage's aliases; he had several when he was waiting around between my soul's various lifetimes, and apparently they all did quite well for themselves. "My uncle said he'd cover the cost," I say, handing over the card and a folded piece of paper. "He sent along a signed letter of permission."

Brightley raises an eyebrow at the card, then compares the signature on the back to the one on the note. I can all but guarantee that as far as he's concerned, Spirit Charlotte will need a *very* long time to make her transition. I told Sage to give me twenty-four hours. If I need more, I'll tell him, but I definitely won't be staying as long as Brightley would hope.

"Wonderful," he says. "Now we have some forms for you to sign. All very routine."

That pretty much guarantees that the forms are *not* very routine, but I soothe myself as I sign by reminding myself I'm not signing my own name, so they can't possibly be binding.

"Excellent. Now Spirit Bitsy can take you to get changed."

We rise from the from the table, and although I didn't see him press any kind of button or alert her in any way, Spirit Bitsy the Sunflower is right there when he opens the door.

"This is it, Spirit Charlotte!" she bubbles. "The beginning of your new life. Let's go."

As she leads me over hardwood floors and under wrought-iron chandeliers, I ask if everyone working at Transitions has transitioned themselves.

"Oh, yes. Spirit Burnham has a beautiful story of how he made his transition. I'm sure you'll hear it; it's very inspirational."

I'm sure it is. "How about you?"

"Before I worked here, I was a transitioner just like you. This body was born with the sprit of Anna, but she couldn't handle living with the difficulties it entailed." She holds up her clawed hands. "Sprit Bitsy was more than happy to work within those confines, and we've both been happier since I've walked in."

"You've both been happier?" I ask. "You've been in touch with Sprit Anna?"

"Oh, no. But I know how badly she wanted to move on, and I'm sure she's now at peace."

Spirit Bitsy reaches into her pocket with her clawlike hands to fetch a key card, which she presses against a panel. An unmarked door springs open to reveal the most unassuming room I've seen yet at Transitions. While the carpet is a luxurious deep pile in an unfortunate shade of baby blue, the room itself holds nothing more than a mirror, a dresser with a shelving unit, and a dress rack. No windows. The shelves are filled with women's flats, all in the exact same shade of blue as the carpet. On the dress rack are six simple sundresses, all that same blue, all the same shape, though they range in size from super petite to extra large.

"The first step in easing Sprit Krysta's way is to give her a blank slate. Spirit Charlotte has been entrenched in this body a long time. Everything about it—the clothes you wear, your accessories, even everything in your wallet—it's all tied to

Spirit Charlotte. So I'll need you to hand over all your possessions, then get changed into whichever dress and shoes fit you best. There are underpants, brassieres, and socks in the drawers. Once we know your sizes, we can stock your closet."

She says this like it's the simplest thing in the world, but there are so many indignities stuffed inside, I don't know where to begin.

"Hand over all my possessions?"

"They belong to Spirit Charlotte. We'll keep them safe, and when Sprit Krysta emerges, she can decide what to do with them."

Unease curdles my stomach. It's not like I'll be turning over a lot. Knowing I'd be undercover, I don't have much with me. My ID, credit cards, and anything else with my name on it is in the glove compartment of our rental car. The only things I brought in my purse were a lip gloss, the black AmEx I already turned over, and my cell phone.

It's losing the cell phone that makes me nauseous. It feels like throwing away my only key to that locked front door—a door "Spirit Burnham" will want to keep closed so he can drain Mr. Steczynski's credit card as much as possible.

To calm me, I think about Sage and let his face

fill my mind. Amazingly, it's his new face I see, not the one I used to know. It's the face I want to be with the rest of my life, and that can't happen unless I find whatever secrets this place might hold.

I give my whole purse to Spirit Bitsy, then at her direction I turn out my pockets so she can see there's nothing there. "I'm sorry if it seems draconian," she says sweetly, "but even the smallest link to Spirit Charlotte can hamper the transition process."

"I understand."

"I remember my first day," Spirit Bitsy says, a hint of mist in her eyes. "It was so overwhelming. But believe me, once you transition, you'll be so much happier. Spirit Krysta will take over all your burdens, and you'll have eternal peace and happiness. I'll be right outside the door. Just knock when you're ready."

She gives my arm a supportive squeeze, then uses her key card to pop open the door. Handles and knobs are apparently at a premium here at Transitions.

I stare at the dress rack.

I hate baby blue.

The underwear I at least expect to be white,

but when I open the drawer, I find another sea of baby-boy pastel. Ugh. As I find my size and pull it on, I can't help thinking about how many other people have worn them, and for a second I can't bear to let it touch my skin. Next I go to the dresses, which run big; I try on two of them before I find the one that fits. It's comfortable, at least; a soft cotton with thick straps over the shoulders and an empire waist. I add the flats and look at myself in the mirror. Aside from the color, it's not a hideous outfit. I guess Brightley figures that with the crazy money people spend on this place, they want their institutional wear to at least smack of chic.

I knock on the door, and Sister Bitsy pops it open immediately, her face aglow.

"You look beautiful," she says. She bags up my regular clothes, makes note of all my sizes, then says she'll lead me to my room. As we go, we walk out the back of the reception building and onto a rock path that winds over the lush lawn, around the pool, and toward a circle of casitas, each three stories tall, with large windows and patios off each level. There are a few more people around the pool, and I notice what I missed before: All their bathing suits are the same shade of powder blue as my dress. I can't fathom how Brightley imagined powder blue would be the perfect "neutral" shade; maybe the dye was on closeout.

Spirit Bitsy calls out hellos as we wander along the path. Then, as we get closer to one of the casitas, I notice a clutch of three women sitting on the patio of the top floor, dressed in tops and shorts splashed with every color *except* baby blue. "Some of the transitioners keep their regular clothes?" I ask Spirit Bitsy.

"Oh, no," she says. "They're facilitators. They've already transitioned, so their new spirits are of course free to personalize their bodies. It also makes them easy for transitioners to spot. If you have any questions; they're the ones to ask. Along with myself and Spirit Burnham, of course."

"Actually, I do have a question," I say. "After you transitioned, did you ever have any problems?"

"What kind of problems?"

"Issues with your new soul. Did your body have any trouble accepting it?"

"Not at all. Why would it?"

"No reason. Just wondering. Have you known any other transitioners to have problems afterward?"

She gives me an understanding smile and puts a gnarled hand on my arm. "It's normal to be worried about the next step, but if you ask me, that's what's holding you back from making the change you want. Let go of your fear. Spirit Krysta will do just fine in your body."

I smile and thank her, but inside I'm disappointed. Either Spirit Bitsy has no experience with soul rejection, or if she does, she won't say anything about it.

She leads me to an outdoor spiral staircase, and we climb to the second floor of the casita next to the one where the facilitators are taking in the sun. Unlike the doors in the main building, this one has a regular knob. "Spirit Charlotte, welcome to the last earthly building that will ever weigh you down, and the first that Spirit Krysta will call home."

She flings open the door to an airy, open apartment. Light streams in from the floor-to-ceiling windows, illuminating every room I walk through. Everything is large and spacious: the kitchenette, living room, bathroom, and bedroom. There's plenty of closet space, which Spirit Bitsy assures me will be filled with a full wardrobe of clothing within the hour.

It has all the amenities of a five-star hotel, but without the technology: no computers, no phones, no TV. Spirit Bitsy says this is so transitioners won't be distracted by the outside world as they prepare to make their change. Before she leaves, she hands me a paper cup with my "vitamin" and tells me to take it right away, then assures me someone will fetch me for my therapy session before dinnertime, but until then I'm free to wander the grounds and relax.

Vitamin. I'd bet any amount of money it's some kind of psychotropic drug to help residents believe they're really "transitioning." I pretend to take it in case there are any Big Brother cameras around, but I actually palm and flush it.

Now to mingle.

I really want to talk to the five facilitators. If any of them had a genuine Walk-In experience, they might have dealt with soul rejection. I go outside and look up at the patio next door, but the three women aren't there anymore. Instead I wander to the pool. It's so hot outside I'm dying to jump in, but my no doubt baby-blue swimsuit hasn't been delivered yet, so I just sit on the side and dangle my feet in the water. Of the ten transitioners, five of them are here at the pool, but the person who catches my eye is an older man with thick white hair and wrinkled flesh that sags off his gaunt build and over the band of his disturbingly small bright-green Speedo.

Bright green. A facilitator.

He walks back and forth in the shallow end, and when he notices me he smiles, showing his yellowed teeth.

"Why, hello!" he says. "You're new here, aren't you? I'm Spirit Angus."

"Nice to meet you," I say. "Spirit Charlotte."

He shakes my hand. His grip is strong, and the life in his dancing blue eyes takes years off his age.

"How long has it been since you transitioned?" I ask.

"Oh, two years now."

"Really? And you've stayed here the whole time?"

"Of course! It's incredibly fulfilling to see the joy brought into people's lives when they transition. And what would I do out there in the world, pay a small fortune for a retirement community? I'd rather spend my nest egg here and give a little something back to Spirits like yourself."

"You don't ever want to go back?" I ask. "What about your family?"

"I don't have any family out there. Spirit Rory did, of course. A wife, close friends . . . but they all passed on, one by one. They take your memories, when they go. When you can't share them with anyone who was there."

He's lost in that past, and it's so easy to picture how painful it must have been.

"I'm so sorry," I say.

"His wife was the worst," Spirit Angus continues. "When he saw her lowered into the ground, under the stone with the blank half just waiting for his own name . . . that's when he was done."

He sits with the memory a moment, then blinks, and the sunshine returns to his eyes. "But that wasn't my life, it was Spirit Rory's. He was terribly depressed, of course, but then I stepped in and offered to take his place, so he could join his loved ones. Now we're both where we're meant to be."

I think about his story, and Spirit Bitsy's wasted hands. I'm understanding more about Transitions now, and I ask the next question with a good sense of what he'll say ahead of time.

"After you transitioned, did you have any problems? Trouble with your memory, sickness . . . anything?"

A transitioner in the Jacuzzi looks up at my question. She looks like she's my age or just a little older, with the body of a swimsuit model, long brown hair, and a perfect tan, and I wonder what brought her here. Despite her beauty, she seems uncertain in her own skin. Her shoulders hunch a little bit, and she lets her hair fall around her like a curtain between herself and the world. She looks away shyly when I catch her eye.

"Spirit Charlotte, the only problems I had were *before* my transition," Spirit Angus assures me. "Trust me, this will be the best thing you've ever done."

I thank him, and he goes back to walking the pool. I want to talk to the transitioner with the long brown hair, but she's already in her towel, scurrying back to her room.

While I don't get to chat with her, the pool is clearly the focal point for socializing at Transitions, and over the next couple of hours, I talk to several more residents, both transitioners and facilitators, and I get it. Everyone here has a sob story, some terrible trauma they can't handle. Listening to the stories, I feel like I'm manning a suicide hotline. People tell me about murdered family members, terrible accidents, debilitating diseases, crippling depression . . . it's gut-wrenching.

Yet somewhere along the way, each of the residents stumbled into the theory of Walk-Ins and jumped on it, creating a new "spirit" that wanted to take over. A spirit that had never experienced the trauma, and could therefore function in the world. Word of mouth led them to Transitions, where the combination of vitamins and therapy let them embrace their new self and eventually return to the world.

I'm glad I've figured this out in time for my therapy session that afternoon. It's in the main building, another key-card-controlled door with another baby-blue pile rug. This room is cozier than the dressing room, though, with a cushy couch, pleasantly dim lighting, and incense that smells, ironically enough, like sage. Despite myself, I relax right away, and fall even more at ease when the therapist, Deborah, introduces herself. She's middle-aged and dresses like an earth mother, in a floor-length black skirt and knitted flowered top. She wears thick, dark-framed glasses, and gray streaks the black curls that cascade down her back. Her voice is hypnotically calm and makes me feel like she'd never judge me, no matter what I say.

Still, when she asks me why I want to move on, I know I have to have a truly tragic story, and it's frightening to realize I don't have to make one up.

"It all started when my father died," I begin, then take her through all the highlights: meeting the love of my life only to have him kidnapped and nearly killed, then rescuing him and thinking everything would be okay . . . when it turned out he had a disease that was destroying his mind, and there might be no cure.

By the time I finish I'm crying, and Deborah gently tells me I can end all that pain by just letting go of myself and welcoming in Spirit Krysta, a whole new soul with none of Spirit Charlotte's baggage. She asks me to sit cross-legged on the floor, and she joins me.

"Close your eyes," she says, "and picture Spirit Krysta. Picture everything about her—how she dresses, how she wears her hair, what she likes to do . . . but most of all, picture her happy and enjoying life in your body, free from all the pain and suffering Spirit Charlotte had to endure."

I close my eyes, and when she thinks I'm picturing it, she taps my knees, one at a time, back and forth.

Tap-tap-tap-tap-tap-tap.

Six times to lock in the image.

I know this technique. I was in therapy for almost a year after my dad died. It's called EMDR, and it's supposed to retrain the brain. I can see how it would work for people like the ones I've met at Transitions, especially if they're taking "vitamins" that make them even more open to suggestion. In some ways, I'm not even sure it's so terrible. The residents I talked to couldn't bear to face another day the way they were; Transitions gives them a way to be happy again. Sure, in a perfect world it would be better if they could do that without creating a whole new persona for themselves, but if the world was perfect, they wouldn't have had the trauma to begin with. And yes, "Spirit Burnham" is a charlatan pretending he believes in Walk-Ins, and he's making a killing off their pain, but in a weird way he's also maybe doing them a favor.

"Okay," Deborah says. "You can open your eyes. How do you feel?"

I look into her kind face and inhale the strong scent of sage . . . and I burst into tears all over again.

"It's okay," Deborah says, pulling me into a hug. "It's okay. It's always hard when you come back to the present, but I promise, Krysta is coming, she is."

I cry even harder because she doesn't understand. Of course she doesn't. I knew we were grasping at straws coming to Transitions, but I really hoped I'd find something that would help heal Sage. Instead all we've done is lose time coming all the way out to Arizona when we could have been doing more research at home.

"It's not fair," I sob. "After everything we've been through, it's not fair. I can't lose him now."

"Spirit Krysta won't," Deborah says. "Spirit Krysta has nothing to lose, so she'll be just fine."

For a second I wish there really was a Spirit Krysta. It would be much less painful to stop caring so much and let a whole new person take over. Then I think of Sage losing his memories, and how tragic it would be to have those memories and throw them away willingly. No matter how much they make us ache, our memories are our lives. How can anyone let them go?

Maybe Brightley isn't doing his residents a favor after all.

With another hug, Deborah sends me off to dinner. I consider trying to get out and head back to Sage, Rayna, and Ben right now, but I have to at least talk to the remaining residents on the off chance one of them has an actual insight into true soul-swapping. I doubt I'll find anything, but I'm here, so I need to make sure. I follow Deborah's directions to the opulent dining room in the main building and hear a wild buzz of excited chatter. I see Spirit Angus at the large dining table, resplendent in black pants and a maroon smoking jacket, and ask him what's going on.

"Oh, Spirit Charlotte, it's wonderful!" he exclaims. "Spirit Lianne is transitioning! If all goes well, she'll be leaving first thing in the morning!"

Have I met Spirit Lianne? I scan the room and quickly pinpoint the one person who isn't here: the shy woman with the long brown hair. I guess when you transition, you can't be bothered with meals.

The only empty seats at the table are between people with whom I've already chatted, but it doesn't even matter, because no one wants to talk about anything except the exit of Spirit Lianne and the imminent arrival of Spirit Maggie.

It's almost enough to make me lose my appetite, but the food is unreal. I remember what Spirit Angus said about how he'd pay the same thing he pays here for a good retirement community. I doubt if any retirement community would feed him as well as this, and my feelings about

Brightley's little venture become ambiguous all over again.

After dinner it's clear the residents still can't talk about anything but Spirit Lianne/Maggie, so I go back to my apartment, where I change into one of the baby-blue nightgowns now stocked in my dresser and lie down. I can see the three-quarter moon shining through the sliding door to my patio, and a single star next to it. Or maybe it's Venus. Doesn't matter; either way I can use its help. I close my eyes and whisper like I did when I was a little girl: "Star light, star bright, first star I see tonight, I wish I may, I wish I might, have this wish I wish tonight." I squeeze my lids tighter and concentrate with all my being. *I wish I could find a way to help Sage.* I wish it into the world until I'm exhausted, and at some point, without knowing it, I fall asleep.

I wake up to a roar of voices. I open my eyes and squint at the first rays of sunlight peering over the pink horizon. I roll out of bed, pull open the patio door, and step into the already hot morning. Spirit Lianne sits in a pool chair surrounded by residents, but it's not Spirit Lianne anymore. This woman wears her hair pulled back into a ponytail, revealing her beautiful face to the world. She sits up straight, her shoulders pulled back, and speaks with animated gestures, laughing loudly and easily. Even her clothes have changed; she's no longer in baby blue, but a red dress with a plunging neckline.

This must be Spirit Maggie, but is she a coping mechanism finally embraced by Spirit Lianne, or is there even a possibility she really is a whole new soul in Spirit Lianne's body? And if so, how is she handling the soul transfer?

There's only one way to find out.

I rummage through my dresser, pull out a pair of baby-blue shorts and a matching tank top, and head out to join the crowd. They're like paparazzi surrounding a celebrity, and I flit around the outside of the circle, trying to figure out what I'll have to do to get a second alone with her.

Turns out I don't have to do anything.

"Stop, stop, stop!" Spirit Maggie waves her hand in the air, and the crowd quiets at her behest. Between the heads of two people between us, I see her eyes lock on mine. "I want to talk to Clea."

A chill runs over my body. How does she know my name?

There's a murmur of confusion among the crowd, then Spirit Angus follows her gaze. "You mean Spirit Charlotte?"

Spirit Maggie smiles and laughs. "Of course. Sorry. New here. I don't remember all the names."

The crowd eats that one up, and parts so Spirit Maggie can walk to me and link her arm through mine. "We'll just need a sec," she calls back to the crowd. "I promise I'll be back to answer all your questions!"

She cuddles my arm closer to hers like we're best friends, and guides me along a path that loops around the back of the casitas.

"Why, Clea Raymond, as I live and breathe," she says. "And I *do* live and breathe." As if to prove it, she takes an exaggerated deep breath, then blows it out with a giggle.

"How do you know my name?" I ask.

"Oh, come on, you really don't recognize me? I suppose I should be flattered. I didn't exactly look my best the last time we met, but several hundred years will do that to a body, isn't that right?"

She looks up at me again, and my heart thuds against my chest as her blue eyes match a memory: those same orbs, milky with cataracts, lolling inside a body mummified with age. My skin crawls and I try to pull away, but she holds me firmly in her grip, just like she did the last time I saw her.

"Magda." It comes out only a whisper.

She clamps my arm tighter. Though her new body is young and vital, I still feel those ancient skeletal claws. "Well done!" she says.

Even her voice is new, but in it I hear that same wicked playfulness with which she tortured Sage and me in Japan. I watched her kill herself there, saw her shatter the glass charm that kept her alive, looked on as her ancient body crumbled to dust. She was dead . . . and now she's back.

"So it's true," I say, stunned. "Brightley really does help people change places with other souls."

Magda throws back her head and cackles like a fairy-tale witch. "Brightley? Burnham Brightley is a con artist. Spirits don't need *him* to shoehorn them in and out of bodies. Anyone who 'transitions' here does it despite him. In the case of my little friend Lianne, this place almost *stopped* her — she enjoyed the 'spiritual energy' so much, she changed her mind about leaving. Do you know how hard I worked to convince her? It nearly destroyed me — I created constant visions and nightmares, twenty-four hours of horror a day, before she finally agreed to vacate."

"You killed her?" I ask, repulsed.

"I *helped* her. She was a troubled girl. In and out of rehab, never happy . . . she didn't *want* to live. How do you think I found her? I was a wandering soul looking for a host. Her pain called to me."

"A wandering soul," I say with grim satisfaction. "I guess you weren't allowed to rest after all."

She laughs again, and it turns my stomach. "That's cute. You think I'm back because of some divine justice. I gave Sage the tools to destroy his soul, so mine was condemned to wander the Earth. No, Clea. I *chose* to come back. I could've had eternal peace. I tried it. But you know what I found out?" She leans close to whisper in my ear. I recoil, but her grip is too strong.

"Eternal peace is boring," she says. "Deathly boring. The living world is far more exciting. Especially in a body like this." She releases me and spins, making her red dress twirl. "I chose well, don't you think?"

"I think you're evil. I feel sorry for Lianne and anyone else you'll meet in this lifetime." I stalk away, but don't get far before her sickly-sweet voice stops me in my tracks.

"Leaving so soon? Before I can help you keep Sage in his new body?"

Her words knock the air out of my lungs. When I turn around, her mouth is twisted in a confident smirk.

"How do you know?" I ask.

"How do you think? I've been right here while Lianne struggled. Everything she did, I did. I saw you asking people questions. I heard you talking to the old man about difficulties after a transition. There are only two reasons I can imagine why you'd do that. I'd like to think you're so lost and depressed over Sage's grisly demise that you want to give up and let another soul take over. But I don't buy it. You're too together; you handle yourself too well. That leaves the other option: Sage used the dagger I gave him, but his soul found a new host. And maybe he's having troubles?"

"I don't want to talk about this with you," I say, but I don't walk away. I don't trust Magda at all, but she's the only person here who truly understands, and I'm transfixed.

"I think you do. Tell me—unlike my dear Lianne, Sage's host didn't choose to leave his body, did he?"

"No."

"And now it's rejecting the new soul. Can't be pleasant for Sage. Or for you, I imagine."

The last thing I want is her fake sympathy. "I'm fine," I say. "Sage will be too."

"No, he won't. Not unless you appease the ancient healers."

"What?"

"I'm telling you what to do. If you want to save Sage, you need to appease the ancient healers."

I have no idea what she means, but it doesn't even matter. "Why would I listen to anything you say?" I ask. "All you ever wanted was for Sage to suffer."

"Not true, Clea. Sage and I were together once . . . or don't you remember?"

"Of course I remember." Before Sage ever drank the Elixir of Life he was with Magda, but he left her for Olivia . . . me in a past life. "It's why you hate him so much."

"Oh, I think you know I have better reasons for hating him than that," Magda says with a condescending laugh. "We both do. He destroyed my life and ended yours. But I'm like you now: I have a whole new body and a whole new life. Don't get me wrong—I'm glad Sage suffered. He deserved it. But it's enough."

I don't know what to say. Does she mean it? I search for the truth in her face, as young and beautiful as it had been in her first life. I see sympathy in her eyes, but can I trust it?

Before I can figure it out, Burnham Brightley's voice rings out. "Spirit Maggie, there you are! We've been looking for you; it's time to leave!"

Magda and I both turn to see Brightley speed-walking toward us, Spirit Bitsy at his side. The rest of the residents follow in a throng close behind.

"Oh look!" Magda chirps happily. "They've all come to say good-bye. How sweet!" She smiles and waves, then starts walking toward them. Panic speeds my heart and I grab her arm.

"Okay," I hiss, "I'm listening. 'Appease the ancient healers.' What does that mean? What do I have to do?"

But Magda isn't listening. She dislodges herself from my grip and stands next to Brightley, smiling for the crowd.

"Spirit Maggie," Brightley announces, "it is my privilege to congratulate you on your successful transition. Your paperwork is complete, and your car service is waiting out front. Shall I escort you to your new life?"

He extends an arm and Magda bats her eyes

flirtatiously as she takes it. "I would be honored, Spirit Burnham."

They head off toward the main building, the other residents closing around them. As they go, Magda looks over her shoulder to me. "Good luck!"

Good luck? No. I need more. I have to know what to do.

"Wait!" I race after her, pushing through the other residents until I can grab her free arm. "Magda! *Maggie!* You can't leave yet. You have to tell me what to do!"

"Unhand Spirit Maggie, Spirit Charlotte," Brightley says, tsking. "It's time for her to go."

I ignore him and lock eyes with Magda. "*Please.*"

Magda winces. "My arm. You're bruising me."

Brightley looks over my shoulder and nods. Immediately, two of the facilitators, a burly man named Andrew and one of the middle-aged women, grab my arms and pull me away from Magda, who keeps walking away with the crowd. I flail wildly, kicking and squirming until my captors' grip loosens enough for me to run back to Magda and throw myself on her, clutching her shoulders and spinning her to face me. "Tell me!" I beg. "If you really want to help, please, *tell me!*"

She nods and leans in even closer. "Seek the Greeks," she says, and it looks like she's about to add more, then her eyebrows furrow at something just over my shoulder. I spin around to follow her gaze . . . just in time to see a man with a syringe.

By then it's too late.

I wake up in a world of fuzzy edges. I'm in bed, and the sun pierces my eyes. It's not the king-size bed from my sprawling Transitions apartment. This is a twin bed, in a small room with a single window high on the wall, vinyl flooring, and a door that sits halfway open, revealing a tiny bathroom.

Where am I?

I try to sit up, but I can't. There are thick bands of fabric over my chest, waist, and legs.

I need to get to Sage. *Appease the ancient healers,* Magda said. *Seek the Greeks.* I don't know what it means, but I'm sure Ben can help me figure it out.

"Hello?" I scream. "Hello? *HELLO?*"

The door opens, and Spirit Bitsy walks in.

"Hello, darling," she says. "I'm sorry about all this, but you were violent, and we had to take precautions. It's for your own safety as well as the safety of the other transitioners."

"I understand." Better to appease her. She'll be more likely to let me go that way. "I'm so sorry. I don't know what got into me, but I'm feeling much better. I need to leave. I need to get out of here. *Now.* I need to go." I'm rambling, but I can't stop. Whatever they shot me with hasn't completely worn off, and I'm not as in control as I need to be.

Spirit Bitsy clucks. "You're still so agitated. Spirit Burnham said we might need to keep you sedated for a few days."

"A few days? No! You can't! I need to leave! Let me talk to Brightley—Spirit Burnham! Please!" I already know what I'll tell him. I'll tell him I'm undercover, that I have no desire to expose him, but my friends are expecting me, and if they don't see me right away, they'll tell the press, and he *will* be exposed. I'll tell him who I really am, so he knows people would listen if a story about me hit the news. He'll know it isn't worth the publicity. He won't even argue. All I have to do is talk to him and tell him. . . .

I feel the sharp stick of a needle in my arm, and soon I can't remember what I want to tell him. I do know the bed is very comfortable, and I don't even mind the restraints. If I relax, I don't even feel them.

I think about Sage. I think he needs me for something, but I can't remember what.

Oh, well. Whatever it is, it can wait. This bed is really so cozy. . . . There's no rush to go anywhere at all.

twelve

RAYNA

Okay, I'll admit it. I've had the occasional bender. I've had nights where I've drunk way too much, gone to bed with the room whirling around me, and woken up in the morning so nauseous I've prayed for an anvil to fall on my head and knock me unconscious and out of my misery.

This morning I feel worse.

What did I do? Did I really tell Ben he should push Sage's soul out of Nico's body?

No. That's saying it nicely. That's taking it easy

on myself. I told Ben he should *kill* Sage. And I gave him what he needed to do it.

I'm totally going to throw up.

I have to talk to Ben and tell him I was wrong. I'll get him to give me back Nico's ring. We'll go ahead with whatever Clea finds out at Transitions, and we'll make Sage okay again.

I'm in the bathroom connecting my room to the guys', my hand on the doorknob, when I hear Nico wail in horrible pain. Like he just found out his soul is doomed to be lost forever. I shake and feel my breath catch in my throat. In a wild panic, I throw open the door and race into Ben and Sage's room . . . where Sage is still howling in Nico's voice, but it has nothing to do with anyone's soul.

"Double skunk!" Ben crows. The two of them sit cross-legged on one of the room's double beds, the cribbage board and cards between them. "Oh, hey, Rayna," he says when he notices me.

I don't answer. I'm still trying to catch my breath and make sense of what I'm seeing. How can Ben sit and play cards with a man he condemned to death? I can't even look at Sage.

"Ben, can I talk to you a minute?"

"Sure!" he says, then he glances at the clock.

"Oh, wait. After breakfast, okay? Whatever Molly made, I don't want the other guests to eat it all before we get down there. You coming?"

The last question he directs to Sage, since I'm still in the tank top and boxer shorts I slept in.

"Your manners are horrible," Sage says, then turns to me. "I'll wait for you, Rayna."

He's being polite. I wish he wouldn't be polite. It reminds me of Nico, whose soul isn't at peace, and might never be at peace unless . . .

"That's okay," I say. "You go ahead."

I go back to my room and try to figure out what to do, but I can't. I keep changing my mind. When I think about Sage dying, it's easy—of course I don't want that to happen. Who wants anyone to die? But then I think about Nico and that's easy too—of course I want his soul to move on. And then I start thinking about Sage's five hundred years compared to Nico's twenty-one and how Nico *never* caught a break while Sage has had so many. . . .

I need a psychic. I need to talk to Nico's soul directly and let it tell me what to do.

No. I don't need a psychic. If Nico's soul is trapped inside Sage, I know exactly what he'd want. He'd want to be set free. But that means destroying Sage . . . and how could I ever look at Clea again if I was partly responsible for her losing the love of her life?

Then again, it's not like she's losing sleep because she's partly responsible for me losing the love of *my* life.

I can't deal. By the time I brush my teeth and get dressed, I'm exhausted again, and I lie back onto the bed. I wake up to the smell of sweet baked dough, and open my eyes to see Nico holding a tray of French toast.

Not Nico. Sage. Having one of his rarer and rarer normal moments, which at the moment is the last thing I want to see.

"Hey," he says. "Breakfast was ending, so I asked Molly if she'd make you a tray."

"Thanks. I . . ."

I realize I have an opportunity. I couldn't reach Nico's soul when I was meditating in the pool yesterday, but if he's really caught in this body, maybe now I have the chance. Maybe I needed to be physically closer. It's worth a try. We *are* in a spiritual vortex.

And then I'd know.

"Can you do me a favor?" I ask Sage. "I've been working on this yoga partner pose. . . . It's really amazing and I'd love to do it here. . . . Would you help me out? It won't take long."

Sage is a little weirded out by the request, but he agrees, so I have him sit on the floor with his legs in front of him, spread slightly apart. I sit across from him, my legs outside his, so his feet are pushing my legs apart. I reach my arms forward and have him grab and pull them until I'm folded over. It's a fantastic stretch, but really it's just an excuse to have Nico's body close to me for a while, so I can concentrate. I take deep breaths, open myself up to the energy of Sedona, of the vortexes, and focus every bit of my being on reaching out to Nico's soul.

An eternity passes. My limbs ache. I can't hold this position much longer, and I'm sure Sage's patience is running thin.

This isn't accomplishing anything.

"Rayna?"

That voice. It's Nico's—the way it sounded before Sage came in and made it rougher somehow. I'm so surprised I almost let go, but I don't. I grab tighter and lift my head so I can look into his eyes.

His *blue* eyes.

Nico's whole face lights up when I meet his gaze. He smiles . . . the same smile he had when he asked if I'd marry him one day.

It lasts only an instant, then he squeezes his eyes shut . . . and when he opens them again they're brown once more. Did I imagine it?

"All stretched out?" Sage asks.

"Yeah," I say. "Thanks. And thanks for breakfast."

"My pleasure," he says. He gets up and extends a hand to help me. I can only stare as he walks out of the room.

I didn't imagine it. It was real. It was a sign. It has to be. Nico's soul—at least part of it—*is* inside that body. I reached it.

Now I have to release it. But if I do, I destroy Sage.

What should I do?

I wrestle with it all morning, then go downstairs to find Ben and Sage stressing about Clea. Transitions has yet to call and say we can visit her. That's a more immediate thing to worry about, so I put my focus there. The three of us keep looking at our cell phones, picking them up, checking the volume and the messages.

By early afternoon, none of us can handle being cooped up. I'm out of the pool, the guys are out of the inn, and we're all trying to stay sane in the yard. Sage paces like a lion, Ben bites his nails, and I attempt to calm myself with yoga, even though I keep toppling over because I can't concentrate on any poses.

"Screw this!" Sage finally snaps. "We should just go drag her out of there."

"Oh yeah," Ben laughs. "Clea's real big on the 'drag her out of there' approach."

"You'd rather we just sit around and wait?"

"No," Ben says. "We've waited long enough. We call. Rayna, you do it. You're the concerned sister."

"I'm the concerned brother!" Sage roars.

"And when you flip out and scream at them like that, I'm guessing they're not going to be so excited about letting us see Clea. Rayna?"

The Transitions number is programmed in my phone.

"Transitions!"

"Hi, Spirit Bitsy! It's me . . ." I completely blank on my fake name. Ben starts humming and doing some weird charades thing. I have no idea what he's trying to say. "Charlotte's sister."

"Oh . . . Clementine . . ."

Clementine. That explains it. He was singing the song and peeling an orange. I never would have gotten that. My way was much easier.

"Yes. My family and I really would like to visit Charlotte. Is now a good time?"

"Now?"

Whoa. That's weird. I know they like their secrecy and all, but she sounds panicky. Why would she be panicky?

"Yeah. We're pretty close by. So now would be great. Maybe in five minutes?"

Ben and Sage can see on my face that something's off. They both lean in close, and I put the phone on speaker.

"I'm sorry. Spirit Charlotte can't have any visitors right now. It's a sensitive time."

"Sensitive how?" Sage asks, and even I jump at the threat in his voice.

"Oh my! Am I on speakerphone?"

Spirit Bitsy sounds even more frightened now, and Ben smacks Sage on the arm. "Yes, you are," Ben says, "but it's okay. We're all here and just . . . eager to see Charlotte and make sure everything's okay. Not that we think it's not okay or anything. . . ."

He winces at his own clumsiness, and I take the call *off* speakerphone.

"Sorry about that. We'd just love to see her, that's all. Maybe we can come by for a couple minutes."

"No." Her voice is brisk now. "I'm afraid that's impossible. Spirit Burnham said we'd call when she's ready for visitors, and that's exactly what we'll do. Your sister signed papers giving us full discretion, and now is simply not an appropriate time. Thank you and good-bye."

"Well done," I say after she clicks off. "You totally spooked her."

"It's not like she was letting us see her anyway," Ben grumbles.

"No, but now we can't even show up there without the whole place freaking out."

"She was hiding something," Sage says. "Clea's in trouble. We need to get her out."

"How?" I ask. "There's no knob on the door. You think they're going to buzz us in?"

We all think about it, then Ben starts nodding. I keep expecting him to pop out with some kind of plan, but he doesn't.

"Are you going to tell us, or are you nodding about something that has nothing to do with Clea?"

"We can get in," he says. "But we'll need help."

Ten minutes later we're in the kitchen talking to Molly, whose wide eyes and forced smile make it clear she doesn't want us to know her true thoughts. "She's at Transitions! How lovely. I'm sure it's doing her a world of good."

"We don't actually believe in that stuff," Ben says. "Neither does Clea. She's a reporter."

"Oh, thank goodness," she says on a whoosh of breath. "We get a lot of those people here. They're so kooky!"

It's a good sign, and when we explain that our reporter friend might be having trouble undercover and we want to help her, it's easy to get her on board. She uses her cell phone to call Transitions, tells Spirit Bitsy a story about her struggle to come to an agreement with Audrina, a spirit who's ready to take over her body, and asks for an appointment to talk. Spirit Bitsy tries to put her off until the next day, but Molly is surprisingly convincing in her sweet-as-pie way and manages a meeting just two hours later. They're the longest hours in history, but eventually they pass, and we all climb into Molly's enormous SUV. When we get close, Ben and I lie flat in the trunk area, while Sage crouches down as best he can in the foot wells of the backseat. We brought along some old blankets, and with them tossed over us, it's unlikely any camera will notice that the car is occupied by anyone other than Molly.

I can't see what's going on at all, but I know the plan. I know when the car slows to a stop that she's pulling as close to the front door as she can without it seeming odd. I hear her open and shut the car door.

"Get ready," Ben whispers. He rises up just enough to see out the window, and I shift to my elbows and put a hand on the latch for the back. If all is going well, Molly's buzzing the intercom, and any second now . . .

"Go!" Ben says.

I pull the latch, and Ben and I leap out the back hatch while Sage races out of the backseat. We storm the front door, where Molly has positioned herself beautifully in the threshold, so a shocked Spirit Bitsy can't close the door on her.

"What are you doing?" Spirit Bitsy asks us.

"Taping," I say, indicating my cell phone camera, which I hold up to get everything. "Smile!"

Bitsy flies at me like a perturbed moth. She tries to grab for the phone, but she can't accomplish it with her gnarled hands, so she just jumps up and down and waves her arms, flitting in front of my lens. "We don't allow photography here!" she squeals. "Stop!"

Sage moves right next to her. He dwarfs her, and I'm not positive, but I think she wets herself a little when he screams down at her, "WHERE IS SHE?"

We hear footsteps, and Burnham Brightley walks in, flanked by two large men holding drawn guns.

"Got the guns on camera, Rayna?" Ben asks.

Oh. Good idea. "Yup, got it!"

Brightley waves his hand, and the guards clip their guns back on their belts. Brightley takes a second to adjust his completely unfashionable — *unforgivably* so with the Birkenstocks — white suit, smooth his blatantly receding hair, and plaster a smile on his face before he strolls toward us. "I'm sorry," he says. "Is there some kind of trouble?"

Sage leaves Bitsy's side to lean on Brightley.

They're actually about the same height, but Sage is far more muscular, and the way all his tendons and veins are popping out has to add another several inches of girth. He's like a less green version of the Hulk.

"We'll make trouble," Sage says. "Where's Clea?"

"Charlotte," I say. "*Spirit* Charlotte."

"Are you threatening me?" Brightley asks. "Spirit Bitsy, please call the police. These trespassers are threatening me."

"I wouldn't do that, Bits," Ben says.

Bits? I roll my eyes. Ben seems to think he's in some kind of old black-and-white detective movie. His voice even sounds weird. Is he trying to do Humphrey Bogart?

"We're reporters," he says. "Call the police and we'll e-mail this video as the start of a huge exposé that'll put you out of business."

Brightley doesn't look particularly worried, but he does give a slight nod to Spirit Bitsy, who takes her hand off the phone. "The only thing your video 'exposes' is your own illegal push onto my property."

With the back of the lobby open to the grounds,

people are starting to walk over and gawk. "What's going on?" asks an old man. He's more wrinkled than a shar-pei and wears a tiny hot-pink Speedo. I get him on camera immediately.

Brightley gives him a smile. "Nothing, Spirit Angus. We were all just about to adjourn to my office."

"No, we weren't," I say. "We like it right here."

"This is all completely uncalled for," Brightley says. "Spirit Charlotte signed papers entrusting us to make her decisions for her. If we don't feel it's in her best interest to see people, that's our prerogative."

"You don't have her signature," Ben says. "Her name isn't Charlotte, it's Clea. Clea Raymond."

If that was supposed to be a bombshell, it's an epic fail. There's not the slightest flash of recognition on anyone's face.

"Her mom's a senator," I say. "Victoria Weston. She's a big deal. The whole family is. You can Google them."

"And Senator Weston will be exceptionally upset if she thinks Clea's being held against her will," Ben says. "I'm talking check-your-tax-records, make-sure-all-your-books-get-audited..."

that kind of upset. Plus, she'd probably look into your program, your accreditation, all those kinds of things. . . ."

The crowd of gawkers has grown, and Brightley looks severely uncomfortable. I'm uncomfortable too, but that's mainly because 90 percent of the people wear a shade of blue that should never be seen outside a baby's room.

"Against her will?" Brightley laughs. "That's absurd. Of course you can see her. Spirit Bitsy? Spirit Bitsy, can you get Miss Raymond? And her things?"

Spirit Bitsy is bent over the computer, but leaps up when he repeats her name. "I apologize. I was just Googling the senator. It's true, she's quite powerful! And to think her daughter's a transitioner!"

I open my mouth to tell her Clea's *not* really a transitioner, but judging by all the excited murmurs from the baby-blue-clad gawkers, that's what they want to run with.

"Just recognize that you're interrupting the transitioning process by seeing Miss Raymond right now, and you may well scare off her burgeoning new spirit forever." He says it to us, but it's totally for the gawkers, who murmur their deep concern.

This place is freaking me out. I want to get Clea and get out of here.

It takes ages, but finally Spirit Bitsy comes back. She has one of Clea's hands pinched between her arthritic fingers and pulls her along like an oversize toddler. A lot like an oversize toddler, since Clea totters on the balls of her feet and looks around at everything with a huge smile on her face.

I don't know what they gave her, but Clea is blitzed.

"Sage!" she screams, and jumps into his arms, wrapping her legs around his waist and her arms around his neck. Then she giggles. "You caught me. I knew you could catch me!"

I'm taping her now, but not for the plan. This is torture material I'll keep with me for the rest of our lives.

"What did you give her?" Sage asks.

"I don't know what you're talking about," Brightley answers, cool as can be.

Sage looks like he's going to eat Brightley alive, but Ben steadies him with a hand on his arm.

"Whatever it is," Ben says, "you'd better hope it wears off without a problem, or you know who we'll be calling."

We pour out of the building, and I'm thrilled when the door to Transitions slams shut behind us. It's not a place I ever want to see again.

thirteen

CLEA

My head throbs. Whatever they shot me with at Transitions left me with a migraine the size of Everest.

I remember everything, though. Even things I don't want to remember, like hurling myself on Sage and clinging to him like a tree frog. Embarrassing. I was a scrambled mess, but I kept it together long enough to tell Sage, Ben, and Rayna all about Magda and what she said.

Appease the ancient healers. Seek the Greeks.

Then I passed out for who knows how long,

and woke up in this room. The stabbing pain in my head was so bad then that I begged them to turn out all the lights and close the blackout curtains, so now I don't know if it's the middle of the day or nighttime.

I feel a million times better. Just a few more minutes lying here with my eyes closed and I'll be able to get moving. We need to go back to Connecticut. Maybe with the clue, Ben can find something in Dad's research, or in the rare books library.

I hear the door open and close. Footsteps. Then a pressure as someone sits next to me on the bed.

"Clea."

It's Sage. His voice soothes the last remaining throb in my head.

"Hey," I murmur. I roll sideways, just a little closer to him, and my skin tingles in anticipation of his touch.

It doesn't come.

He hasn't left the room. I can feel him there next to me.

I open my eyes.

"Sage?"

It's dark, but I can see him staring down at me.

"Hey," I murmur.

He doesn't answer. He's looking at me, but it's almost like he's looking *past* me. He reaches toward my face, and my whole body wants to recoil. He picks up a strand of my hair and examines it . . . like a lion checking out its kill.

Where are Ben and Rayna?

He's gotten worse. . . . I know he can be dangerous. . . . Should I scream?

He lets my hair slip through his fingers, then slides a single finger down my cheek. "Clea," he says again, but there's no love behind it. No emotion at all. He's tasting the word, rolling it over on his tongue.

His finger slides down into the hollow of my throat, and he presses down the littlest bit. Just enough to hurt.

"Sage . . ." I say it softly. I want to bring him back, not set him off. "Please stop. That hurts."

He stops the pressure, but slides his whole hand over my throat. It rests there, not pushing . . . but not lifting, either. "Why shouldn't I hurt you? You want to hurt me."

"I don't. I want to help you. I want to make you better."

"I don't believe you. I think you want to steal my soul. You and your friends. That's what you want to do." His voice is kind, which makes it worse. His hand tightens around my throat, and by the time I decide to scream, I can't.

"Sage . . . ," I croak.

His fingers dig deeper, squeezing my windpipe. He leans close to my face, close enough that I can make out his eyes. They're not Sage's rich brown or Nico's crystal blue. They're green and muddy.

"I can't let you hurt me," he whispers.

I poke him in the eye, hard. He screams, his grip slackens, and I roll off the bed. I scramble out of the room and slam the door behind me to buy a little time. I don't know this inn. I don't know what's around. I turn one corner, then another, then I see a staircase and make a beeline for it. I'm halfway down, looking over my shoulder for Sage, when I slam into a worried-looking Ben and Rayna.

"We heard someone scream—what happened?" Rayna asks.

Another scream seems to answer, and Sage staggers around the corner, one pink eye swelling, the other locking on me murderously. He *growls* when he sees me, and lunges over the railing, arms straining to reach me.

"Stop!" I scream.

"Is everything okay up there?" a woman's voice calls.

"Fine, Molly!" calls Rayna, as Ben races up the stairs and tackles Sage around the ankles. The blow comes out of the blue for Sage, and he falls like a tree. His head slams so hard on the wooden floor that it echoes through the inn.

"Are you *sure* everything's okay up there?" the woman calls again from downstairs.

"Great, Molly!" Rayna chirps.

A soft, high-pitched moan escapes from Sage as he rolls to his side and curls into the fetal position. I scramble to him, but Ben intercepts me. He grabs my shoulders. "Are you okay?"

"I'm fine," I snap impatiently. I brush his hands off me and kneel at Sage's head. He cradles his face in his hands, and his back lurches up and down. The sight is so foreign to me I can't believe it's real, but it is. He's crying uncontrollably, and that scares me even more than his hands around my throat.

"Sage . . . Sage, it's okay. Everything's okay."

He doesn't answer. He can't. I nod to Rayna, and of course she understands. She taps Ben on the arm and leads him downstairs. A minute later

I hear her leading a cheery conversation with everyone else in the inn.

I stay with Sage in the hall, comforting him as best I can until the sobs die down.

"Sage?"

"I remember," he says in a voice barely above a whisper. "I know what I did."

"It wasn't you," I assure him.

"It doesn't matter . . . I could have . . ."

"You didn't. You wouldn't. Even if you would, you *won't*. I saw Magda, remember? You'll get better. Ben's going to figure out what she meant, and you'll get better."

"You really think we can trust Magda?"

It's a question I keep asking myself too. I've run over our conversation again and again in my mind, each time trying to look deeper into her eyes and see the truth.

"I think we're running out of time," I finally say, "and she's the best chance we have."

Sage doesn't respond right away, and I'd give anything to know what he's thinking. With a deep sigh he eventually sits up, but keeps his back to me.

"Could you give me a little time?" he asks. "I need to be by myself."

Now I do know what he's thinking. Fear ripples over my skin, but I won't let it take over. If he's broken, then I have to be strong enough for both of us.

"No. I know you too well." I walk around Sage and plop myself cross-legged in front of him, then duck low so he's forced to meet my eyes. "You think you could hurt me, and you'd rather die than let that happen. You tried that when you were much harder to kill; there's no way I'm letting you try it now."

He looks at me willingly now, his mottled face slack with defeat.

"I love you, Clea."

"And I love you. Enough to tell you that killing yourself doesn't make you noble, it makes you a fool. It spits in the face of everything we have, and the future we're so close to getting. I don't care if I have to handcuff myself to you, I'm not letting you do it."

A hint of a smile curls Sage's mouth. "Handcuffs? That could be fun."

I lean forward and kiss him. He resists at first, then wraps his arms around me and pulls me close. His hands tangle through my hair, rub down my back, snake beneath my shirt. I hear his breath in ragged gasps . . . and then I pull away with a smile.

"The rest comes later. Something worth living for."

Sage gives me his sidelong smirk, then gets up and starts walking down the hall. "I'm going to go lie down for a bit. Maybe you should come with me. You know, just to make sure I don't do something rash."

I roll my eyes, but I do follow him into one of the bedrooms, and we lie in each other's arms until it's time to leave for the airport. Ben booked us on a flight home, where I have confidence we'll figure out how to use Magda's message to save Sage's soul.

Soon, though. It has to be soon.

fourteen

CLEA

Sage is fine the whole ride on the plane. We're not with Ben and Rayna; the plane was pretty full when we booked, so they're several rows behind us and way on the other side. Since the layout is two-five-two, Sage and I have a little section all to ourselves, like a love seat. An ill-conceived love seat with clunky armrests and barely any space (the upgrade I wanted was sold out), but a love seat nonetheless. We watch the same TV shows on our back-of-the-seat screen, counting down

"Three . . . two . . . one" each time we start one so we're in sync and laugh at all the same times. We hold hands, I rest my head on his shoulder . . . It's a bubble of normal in the middle of all our madness. At one point a white-haired woman in the row next to us leans over and asks, "College sweethearts?" Sage immediately says yes, and we spend a half hour telling her stories about our life on campus and our romantic history. We each put in random tiny details, like how we met during a Psych 101 lab, when my lab rat got loose and Sage helped me catch it. All completely fabricated, but for the few hours of the flight, it feels like real life.

It's only after we land, in the car on the way home, that things change. I'm in the back with Rayna, and Sage is in the passenger seat. I can see him gripping the chair, white-knuckled. He's pale, and a sheen of sweat covers his face and forehead. It reminds me of the first drive I took with him in his new body, and I wonder if he's going to get sick.

I lean forward and reach up to rest my hand on his. "Sage . . . ?"

"I'm good, Clea," he says. The words come out in a rush, like he needs to push them out before he runs out of energy. I sit back in my seat and look to Rayna, asking her with my eyes if she sees what I see, and she tells me wordlessly that she does, and she doesn't like it. Ben, on the other hand, looks so sunny I half expect him to break into song.

"Mind if I turn on the radio?" he asks as he goes ahead and does it. He whistles along with the music.

"You're in a good mood," I say.

"Because I have good news," he says. "Or I think I'll have good news. I'm not positive, but I might know what Magda meant. I need to do a little more research, but I think I know where to look. If I'm right, and I can find what I need . . . we might be able to stop the soul rejection tonight."

"Tonight?" I'm so shocked, I don't know what to think.

I turn to Rayna, but she looks so worried I start to wonder if tonight is too soon and something could go wrong. We need to move quickly, though, and if tonight's even possible . . .

"Rayna?" I say. "I think this is good."

Rayna nods, but she doesn't look convinced. I understand. She doesn't want me to get my hopes up too high. But hope is all I have right now, and I need to cling to it. I lean forward and squeeze Sage's shoulder. "Did you hear that?" I say encouragingly. "This could all be finished tonight."

Sage nods, but infinitesimally. The muscles in his jaw clench and unclench as he grips the seat and stares straight ahead.

It's happening again, but he's trying to fight it. My stomach clenches as I imagine him losing control in the car. I can see it like it's real: He lashes out at Ben, who loses control of the steering wheel, and the car swerves wildly into oncoming traffic.

I squeeze my eyes against the fireball exploding in my head, then meet Ben's eyes in the rearview mirror.

"Drive fast, okay?"

He does—so fast I'm amazed we don't get pulled over. I undo my seat belt and lean forward, poised to jump on Sage if he makes any sudden movement. I spend the whole trip that way, never taking my eyes off Sage, every muscle in my body tense and ready to go, but nothing happens.

Ben doesn't even park the car when we get to

my house, just idles long enough for us to get out, then zooms off to New Haven to hit the rare book archive. I wrap my arms around him as best I can from the backseat before I get out. "Thank you," I say. "Good luck."

He drives off, and the three of us blink in the early-morning sun. Rayna yawns and stretches in such an exaggerated way she looks like a cartoon of sleepiness. "I'm super tired," she sighs. "I'm going to go lie down."

She heads to her house and I almost stop her — something's definitely on her mind — then Sage grips my upper arm so hard it hurts. I wheel around, ready to defend myself, but he's not attacking. He's deathly pale, and I can feel the vibration of his trembling muscles.

"I need help," he says, his voice strained and tight. "Help me."

I start to panic. "What can I do?"

"I can feel it, Clea. The rage. I feel . . . wild. I'm trying to hold it back, but I can't much longer . . . and I don't know what it'll do."

When I look into his eyes, I see flecks of green breaking through the brown irises. I don't understand what's happening. Is it a sign of Nico's body pushing out Sage's soul for good? Is tonight already too late to save him?

"Don't let me hurt you," he begs.

"I won't."

He shakes his head, a small movement that strains against his tensed neck muscles. "Not good enough. If you won't let me do what I should . . ."

"Don't even talk like that. You heard Ben. You can be better by tonight. A few hours, that's all you need."

"Then *stop* me. Drug me. Knock me out. You have to. If you don't . . ."

His whole body trembles violently. He tilts his face to the sky and lets out an awful scream that shakes me.

He wasn't exaggerating. He's being eaten alive, and it's only a matter of time before this thing destroys him. I don't know if knocking him out will stop his soul from being rejected while we wait for Ben, but I can't let him go on like this. I grab Sage's hand, and I'm grateful he lets me pull him inside. He's still winning the battle inside him right now, but it's hard-fought. He's breathing heavily, hunches over as he walks, and the sweat is thick on his body. I bring him to my bed, then run to the bathroom and rummage through my medicine cabinet.

Do I have anything that can knock him out? I sift through tubes and bottles, checking out every old prescription bottle I've neglected to throw away. I finally find some Vicodin, from when I had my wisdom teeth out. I shake the bottle. I didn't take much of it; there's still a lot left. Hopefully they're still good; they have to be about two years old. I fill a cup with water and run back to my bedroom.

Sage lies flat on the bed, staring at the ceiling. His breath is shallow and comes in gasps. His skin has turned to parchment. His hands clench and unclench at his side.

Is he even there anymore? Can I still reach him?

He doesn't acknowledge me as I walk to the bed. Slowly. I want to get this in him right away, but I don't want to startle him.

I place my hand on his arm, and his whole body—the whole stiff-as-a-board horizontal expanse of him—flies up in a full body spasm, then flops back on the bed. I want to run. I'm terrified of what he could do, but I have to try and help him.

"Sage . . . I found something . . ."

He turns his head to me, those impossible flecked irises glaring, his mouth and jaw working in a silent struggle. I think he might lunge at me, and I tense up, waiting for the attack. He lashes out . . . and in a single motion sits up, grabs the medicine bottle, rips off the lid, and shakes the pills into his mouth.

"Sage!"

I pull the bottle away as he swallows them dry. How many? I look inside the bottle. I don't know exactly how many were there, but six are left. I rattle them around in the bottle, and the sound is weak. There must have been twice as many before. Did he take six? Will that kill him?

Sage stares at the ceiling again, and his voice is little more than a hiss when he speaks.

"Leave me alone," he says. "Just in case."

I don't know if he means just in case he dies, or just in case the pills don't work and he loses control, but either way, I'm not leaving. I lean against the wall and slide down, where I watch him shake and thrash . . . then settle into an eerie calm that looks like death. I start crying, and I don't want to get up and find out the truth, but somehow I do.

He's not dead. He looks it, but I can feel a soft pulse in his neck, and when I lay my face next to his, I can feel the littlest puff of breath.

The tears come harder, but they're tears of relief. Now we just have to wait for Ben. And hope that whenever Sage wakes up, his soul is still there to be saved.

fifteen

RAYNA

I told Clea I was tired, and I am, but there's no way I can sleep. From the minute I saw Sage go after Clea at the inn, I knew getting him out of Nico's body was the right thing to do. It's not just about giving Nico peace. That would be selfish. It's for Clea's own good too. Sage was like a wild animal. How could Clea ever trust him again, even if Ben could turn back the soul rejection? Maybe it would have worked before, but now Sage is too far gone. He's not just a soul in Nico's body anymore, he's more like an evil spirit. Getting him out is a good thing. It's a service. Like an exorcism.

Ben said it could happen tonight. Nico's soul will be freed, and Sage's soul . . . It'll be freed too! They'll both move on. It's what they both deserve. Peace, and whatever comes beyond this world.

My whole body feels fluttery, like I forgot something important and can't figure out what it is. I can't settle into anything. I try doing yoga in my room, but I get distracted by everything: pictures of Nico and me, pictures of Clea and me, the mess on top of my desk.

The mess on top of my desk has to go. It's a leaning mountain of clothes, old homework assignments, books, makeup . . . Is that my black suede boot? I've been looking for that forever!

I dive into the mess and try to organize it, my head dancing with images of organizational nirvana. I'll put my books in the bookshelf, put all my clothes away, maybe go through and get rid of things I never wear anymore . . .

But if I'm going to clean, I really need to listen to music.

I jump to my iPod docking station and hit shuffle, but as long as I'm here, I should really take the time to flip through and see what I have on this iPod. I haven't synced it with iTunes in ages. Maybe I should do that now?

Ugh!

I shake out my entire body, head to toe.

I can't concentrate!

I grab my phone and text Ben. Whenever it is, I want to be there.

I plop down on my bed and wait for him to text back.

Done.

Relief floods over me.

That was it. If Nico's soul is going to be freed, I need to be there to feel it. I need to reach out to him with every bit of energy in my body and let him know this is my gift to him. This will be my way to tell him I love him, thank him for everything we had, and say good-bye.

That's better. Now I can sleep.

"Rayna!"

Did a giant cat just pounce on my bed? No, I don't have a cat. What is that?

"Rayna, wake up!"

I open my eyes and scream before I realize it's Ben, plopped on the side of my bead, leaning over me with a wild grin on his face. I smack him with a pillow.

"What are you doing?! Who said you could come into my room?"

"Your dad let me in. I figured it out!"

"You figured out why my dad let you in?"

"The way to release Sage's soul. To get him out of Nico's body for good."

A chill races over me, and I hug the pillow tight. "How?"

But Ben's eyes have drifted to the Nico portion of my wall. "Is that a sugar cube?"

"Ben! I'm asking you about the exorcism!"

"The exorcism?"

"Yes! Blasting a bad spirit out of someone else's body. That's an exorcism, right?"

"Okay . . . sure. But an exorcism is usually connected to Christianity. Magda told us to seek the Greeks, remember? Those are the gods whose help we need."

"So . . . we just call up Mount Olympus and ask Zeus and the gang for a solid?"

Ben raises his eyebrows.

"What? I know mythology. I saw *Clash of the Titans*. Even the old cheesy one."

"No. 'Zeus and the gang' won't help us. We need specific gods. Magda also said, 'Appease the ancient healers.'" He leans down, picks up a satchel he'd dropped next to the bed, and pulls out five small geodes — rocks bursting with colorful spiked crystals. He lays them out on the bedspread, one by one: blue, lavender, orange, pink, and green. "Agate, fluorite, wulfenite, calcite, and malachite," he says, "the gem representatives of Panacea, Hygeia, Iaso, Aceso, and Aglaea, the sister goddesses of healing. Invoked properly, these goddesses will stop the soul rejection and secure Sage in Nico's body."

"Wait — I thought we were kicking Sage out of Nico's body."

"Tell me: In your dedicated study of Greek mythology on the IMAX screen, did you learn anything about Eris?"

"Was he played by Ralph Fiennes?"

"No. *She* is the goddess of discord. She's not in the top pantheon, but she's very strong — much stronger than the healing sisters." He reaches into the satchel and pulls out one more geode. The crystals inside this one are jet-black and jut out like blades. "Magnetite. Symbol of Eris. Bring her into the mix and she'll make sure the ritual fails."

"Then Nico's soul can move on and find peace?"

"I believe it can. Yes."

I stare at the geodes, their crystals winking back the light in the room. The Eris crystal is sharpest, and I picture its daggers slicing into Nico's body and tearing Sage's soul away.

"Will it hurt?" I ask.

"Will it hurt Sage? I don't know . . . but I don't think so."

I can't take my eyes off the black crystal.

"Promise me we're doing this for the right reasons. We're doing it because it's the only way Nico's soul can rest, not because it hurts too much to see Clea with her soulmate . . . when neither one of us can be with ours."

I feel Ben stiffen next to me, but when I meet his eyes, he relaxes and runs his hands through his hair. He even laughs a little. "I don't know what you're talking about."

"Ben, you've always been in love with Clea."

"I'm over it." His voice is cold and flat, then he takes a deep breath and lets it out in a tortured sigh. "I'm doing this for Nico. I killed him, Rayna. I think about it all the time, every day. I pushed him to the ground, and he landed on a knife that cut him open."

"Don't . . ."

"I have to. You need to understand. His blood

is on my hands. The least I can do is free his soul.
I can't live with the alternative."

I'm nodding, agreeing before I'm even aware
of it.

"Okay," I say. "Let's do it."

sixteen

CLEA

For the first several hours after he takes the drugs, Sage is deathly still. I stay at his side and watch him sleep. I want to check his pulse and breath constantly, but I force myself to watch the clock and wait. Every fifteen minutes I let myself check. Every time he's alive, but I have no idea if underneath the haze he's still himself or some soulless monster.

As the heavy dose of Vicodin wears off, Sage starts thrashing in bed. Just spasms at first—a leg or arm springing out for just a second. They're like missiles, and I step away from the bed so I don't get hit.

"It's okay, Sage," I tell him. "You can relax. It's okay."

If he hears me, it doesn't show. The thrashing gets worse until his whole body twists and turns so violently I worry he'll dislocate his hip or shoulder. He moans, too, a horrible, agonized wail that I can't bear to hear.

"It's okay!" I say, shouting so he can hear me over his own cries. I feel so helpless, I'm crying too. I can't even get near him, the thrashing is so bad. "Please be okay. Please!"

He bolts upright, eyes wide open, and we both scream.

He's still for a moment, and I see his flecked eyes are more green than brown now. I'm in his sight line, but he doesn't acknowledge me. I don't know if his eyes even see.

Suddenly he bends his legs and grabs around his calves. He rocks back and forth, his voice keening a high-pitched note that doesn't stop.

Oh my God, what is happening?

The note gets higher and higher pitched, like a teakettle ready to burst. He's going to explode if I don't do something. What can I do?

I lunge for the Vicodin bottle and shake it to get his attention.

"Sage? Sage, please, this will help you. Take these. It'll calm you down. You can rest. It'll be okay."

I have the water I brought in before, the water he didn't use when he spilled the pills into his mouth. I tiptoe carefully to his side, on alert in case he lashes out with an arm or leg, but it doesn't happen. I perch on the bed right next to him and hold out the pills and water. For the first time he acknowledges me, his eyes shifting to the side to take me in.

"Take these," I say. I force myself not to cry anymore — not right now — but I can feel the tears behind my eyes. Maybe the pills will help, or maybe they'll put him over the edge into a coma. Or kill him. But the torture in his body is killing him too; I don't have any other options. "Go ahead. It'll be okay. I promise."

Sage's nose flares and every muscle tightens, like he's fighting to gain control. In a rapid swoop, he grabs the pills and water, downs the rest of the bottle, then throws the pill bottle and cup to the floor. He goes back to hugging himself and rocking . . . but then he settles back into that sleep that looks like death. I collapse on top of him and cry until I have no more tears. I feel so out of control and sick. I'm so spent I almost fall asleep, but I remember his flailing limbs and drag myself onto the rug, where I curl up and close my eyes.

The knock on my door makes me scream.

"It's us. Ben and Rayna," Ben says.

I stagger to the door and open it. The two of them wear matching blank expressions, and Ben has a satchel slung over one shoulder.

"I know what to do," Ben says. "We can go right now."

"Go? Where?"

"Boston Common."

"What? Why?"

"I'll explain in the car."

I look at Sage, and they follow my gaze. There's no way he's getting up to go anywhere.

"We have to carry him," Ben says.

It takes all three of us, and we have to stop several times, but we get Sage to Ben's car and wrangle him into the backseat. I slip in too and rest his head on my lap.

"Why Boston Common?" I ask when Ben starts driving.

"Magda's message: Seek the Greeks, appease the ancient healers. We're going to invoke the ancient Greek goddesses of healing, and we have to do it in a place that's sacred to them."

"Boston Common is sacred to Greek gods?"

"You'd be surprised. There was an oak tree there. It's gone now, but in the 1600s and 1700s, it was a big spot for public hangings, many of them for blasphemy. Specifically, they hung people dedicated to the pagan gods, like the Greek pantheon. Even now, the area around that tree is supposed to be filled with the energy of souls ripped away before their time. Souls who gave their lives for the ancient gods. We need that energy to make the ceremony work."

"But you said the tree isn't there anymore," I remind him. "Boston Common's big. How do we know exactly where to go?"

"Your dad knew," Ben says. "It's the kind of thing that fascinated him. He and I talked about it a long time ago. He even took me there a couple times, so I know it. What I didn't know was how to invoke the healing goddesses, but I figured out today. It wasn't easy. Their mythology isn't usually tied to spiritual healing. I never would have known to even look at them if you hadn't found Magda."

So Magda did come through for Sage in the end. Hopefully we won't run out of time before what she told us can help.

We don't talk a lot for the rest of the ride. I concentrate on Sage, cradling his head, wiping the hair off his brow. He stirs every now and then, but there's none of the wild flailing like before. I choose to believe that's because the drugs are helping him rest, not because he's slipped beyond our reach. I run my hands over his face and imagine him waking up with his soul intact and untroubled, a normal human being. I hold tight to that thought and don't let my mind wander.

It's dark by the time we get to Boston Common. Ben parks close to the park and shoulders his satchel, and he and Rayna help me drag Sage out of the car. I feel better once we get past the streetlights and into the unlit Common. The three of us dragging Sage's unconscious bulk isn't exactly inconspicuous. Ben and I are under his shoulders, while Rayna holds his legs. We either look like the casualties of a college kegger, or the most harebrained Mafia body dump ever. We bob and weave as Ben directs us across the park, and it only gets harder when Sage starts to stir. The first flail of his forearm smacks Ben in the cheek, and he almost drops him.

"That's it over there," Ben finally says as we climb onto a low rise. "Let's put him down."

We do it just in time. A wild tremor sends Sage's whole body into spasm, and we all jump away. It settles as fast as it began, but I know we're running out of time before he wakes up completely. And I don't have any more pills.

I look around, but in the moonlight I can't make out anything special about the spot. A stretch of field, the rise of grass, a copse of trees.

"So none of these trees is the oak?"

"No. It was torn down a long time ago. But right here, where Sage is . . . This is where it used to be. Now I just need a couple minutes."

I want to sit with Sage and hold him, but he's not in control of himself. If this goes well—when this goes well—there will be plenty of time to hold him. Instead I move next to Rayna, her curls whipping her face in the light wind. She's pale in the moonlight. When she looks at Sage as he is now, who does she see?

I take her hand. "It'll be okay," I assure her. She doesn't respond at all for a minute, but then she squeezes my hand, never taking her eyes off Sage and Ben.

Ben pulls five colorful geodes from his bag. He says they're agate, fluorite, wulfenite, calcite, and malachite. Each one represents a different healing goddess: Panacea, Hygeia, Iaso, Aceso, and Aglaea. He arranges the geodes in a pentagram around Sage. Then he takes out a notebook . . . and something else. A ring. A gold ring.

"What's that?" I ask.

"A token to appease the host body," Ben says. "I got it from Rayna."

Tears run down Rayna's face. I step closer to her, my arm pressing against hers.

Sage moans, a low, deep groan.

Hold on, Sage. I close my eyes and try to send him my strength. Just a little bit longer.

"Okay," Ben says. "Let's try this."

He stands as close to Sage's head as he can without being in the line of fire and starts reading from the notebook, chanting words I don't understand. Is it ancient Greek? It must be. It goes on for what feels like several minutes. Then he raises his voice, holds the ring over his head, and shouts out the names of the ancient healing goddesses.

Their geodes begin to glow.

Ben grins. He walks to the blue stone — the

agate — at the head of the pentagram and touches the ring to it.

I gasp as slowly, ever so slowly, a thin blue tendril of light reaches out and stretches toward the lavender-crystalline geode. It's beautiful, but I can't believe it's happening.

Ben reaches into his satchel and pulls out one more geode. It's jet-black, with wicked spikes inside. Ben touches the ring to the black crystals, then raises them both in one hand while he chants more Greek from the notebook.

The thin blue light laces with inky blackness. The beam meets the fluorite on one side, and emerges out the other, lavender stained with black, slowly moving toward the next gem, the orange wulfenite. Lavender to orange, orange to pink, pink to green . . . The laser-light path moves faster and faster as it travels, each thin stream of colored light stained with swirling black. It's mesmerizing . . . but it makes me uneasy. It reminds me of an oil spill. Or the colors flecking in Sage's eyes.

I don't like it.

I want to stop the ceremony. Now. Magda lied to us. She didn't want to save Sage at all. She wanted to torture him, just like before.

I open my mouth to scream . . . but I catch myself before I make a sound. I'm being irrational. Sage was already being tortured; he was already being destroyed. Magda didn't have to do anything to make that happen, and she knew it.

Right now Sage's soul is barely hanging on, and this ceremony is the only thing standing between him and oblivion. If I second-guess it and stop it now, there's no way he can survive long enough to try again.

I force myself to watch Sage and not the lights. He rests peacefully. He looks calm, not tortured. I take a deep breath and let it out slowly, willing him to heal with every ounce of my being.

Out of the corner of my eye I see the beam of green and black has almost reached the head of the pentagram, completing the circuit.

Sage's body goes rigid. He screams, then folds into the fetal position.

"SAGE!" I shriek. "Ben, what's happening? You're hurting him!"

But when I see Ben's face I know. He's smiling — a wide, soulless smile I know from other lifetimes, when Ben's soul destroyed us again and again.

No. God, no. The Elixir is gone. The cycle is supposed to be broken. This can't be happening.

"It's almost over!" Ben says in a high, shrill voice. "A couple more seconds and everything will be all ov—"

He doesn't finish. Rayna's red hair flies behind her as she leaps into the pentagram and slams into Ben, tackling him to the ground.

seventeen

RAYNA

I wish I hadn't read his notebook.

I saw it when Ben was in the bathroom, before we went to get Clea. It had fallen out of his satchel. I didn't plan to flip through it. I was just going to put it back.

But something told me I had to check it out.

I knew what it was. Clea had told me Ben was keeping notes on all his research, adding her own observations, using it all to try to find a way to stop the soul rejection and save Sage.

That's not what was there at all. There were

notes, yes. And all kinds of research. But everything Ben wrote was about finding ways to get Sage's soul out of Nico's body, not to help Nico, but to get rid of Sage forever. The worst part was the words scrawled in huge dark pen strokes and underlined three times: "Convince Rayna Nico's soul is in danger to get personal item!!!"

I was livid.

Right after I read that, I heard Ben coming back, so I quickly slipped the notebook back in the satchel and acted like I'd never seen it, but it was all I could think about as we went to Clea's and drove to Boston Common.

Ben only told me the story of Nico's soul being trapped inside his body so he could get the ring. Did Ben even realize it was true? Maybe . . . but maybe not.

And yet it *is* true. I connected with Nico's soul in Sedona. Part of it *is* trapped in Sage's body and deserves to be set free.

But is this ceremony the way to free him? What if it destroys Sage's *and* Nico's souls? Or what if I stop the ceremony, and that destroys the last chance for Nico's soul to move on?

I don't know anymore. I have no idea what's the right thing to do. I feel all alone.

I look at Ben.

He's smiling.

Smiling.

Ben might have Nico's blood on his hands. He might even know Nico's soul is in torment. But that's not why he's doing this. He's doing it because he's still in love with Clea, and he can't have her as long as Sage is alive.

And me? Am I really trying to do the right thing? Or is it just too painful to see Nico's body with someone else, when I can never have his soul?

Oh God. Sage is going to die, and he's going to die because of me.

"You're hurting him!" Clea screams.

That's when I run, as fast as I can.

Ben says something, but I don't hear it. I just run. I jump over the blue-and-black light and into the pentagram, diving for his legs. He's not expecting it, and he tumbles to the ground. The impact knocks the black geode out of his hands, but it's still inside the pentagram, and the final ray of light is still racing to complete the circuit. When the green/black light hits the blue agate, it will be over. Sage will be gone, and I'll have killed him as surely as if I'd stabbed him in the heart.

"What are you doing?" Ben says. The geode is only a few feet away, and he crawls on all fours to get it. I have to stop him, fast, and I only know one way.

I stand up and kick him between the legs as hard as I can.

Ben goes down screaming, and I run to the geode and throw it out of the pentagram.

Instantly, the colored beams of light cleanse themselves of the black. They're crystal clear now—blue, lavender, orange, pink, and green— and as the green beam of light reaches the agate to complete the pentagram, I'm surrounded by a rainbow of light.

It's not just light, though. It has weight, and vibrates with energy. I hear voices—male, female, young, and old—and I somehow know they're the voices of the people who lost their lives in this spot. They laugh, talk, and sing, and even though I can't make out what they're saying, I can feel the emotion. They're happy.

The slightest shadow of a single face stands out in the blur of color.

"Nico."

I can see him, that shadow of his soul that was trapped. I see him smile, the same smile I saw in

Sedona. I reach out to touch his face, but he has all the substance of a trick of the light. He smiles sadly when I pull my hand away, but I know he's sad for me, not himself. He's free. I shake my head and smile, because I don't want him to feel bad. I'll miss him, but I'll be okay.

"One day," I tell him.

His smile broadens, and his face moves toward mine like he's going to kiss me. I lean in for it, but his lips don't meet mine. As it touches my skin, the entire rainbow swirl of his face morphs into sparkles of white, then dissolves.

He's gone.

eighteen

CLEA

Everything happens so fast. Rayna's in the pentagram tackling Ben, they struggle, then I see all the black muddiness disappear from the colored lights. A second later the pentagram outline is complete, and the entire shape is filled with beautiful rainbow colors. Rayna, Ben, and Sage are all inside. Are they okay? What's happening?

I walk to the rainbow wall and put my hand on the edge of the light. I feel . . . happiness. Lost souls finding their way home. Not that I have any idea what that would feel like, but I somehow just know that's what it is. I feel drawn inside, like I could dive in and be part of their happiness, but even though the wall is only light, it's solid.

Slowly, the light recedes. It releases Rayna first. She stands near the top of the pentagram, and she sobs through a smile.

Next the light recedes past Ben. He lies on the ground with his hands over his groin, and I know how the fight with Rayna ended.

Finally the rainbow is entirely gone . . . except for a cocoon around Sage. It hovers around him, pulsing with energy until it disappears underneath his skin, leaving only . . .

It's Nico's body, and for agonizing moments it's perfectly still. Was Rayna too late?

Slowly, the man pushes himself up so he's sitting on the grass. He moves with fluid confidence, the way he did from the first time we met in my dreams. He rolls his neck and stretches his hands over his head.

Then he sees me and flashes the sidelong smile that makes me melt.

I run to him and throw myself into his arms, and he laughs as we tumble backward.

I stare into his eyes, those rich, brown, soulful eyes. "It's you," I say. "You came back to me."

"Forever," he says, and seals it with a kiss that promises everything we ever wanted.

epilogue

CLEA

"Seriously? It's freezing out there. Come inside." Sage stands behind our screen door, his arms wrapped around his body against the New York winter chill.

"Are you kidding? I haven't seen her in *six months*! That's half a year! That's like a lifetime!"

He's not wrong; it *is* freezing, but I'm dressed for it in my parka, scarf, gloves, mittens, and boots. I don't know how long it'll take the cab to get Rayna to our little Brooklyn Heights brownstone in this weather, but I want to be here when she pulls up.

"It's not *quite* a lifetime," Sage says. "And it's not like you don't Skype with her every day."

"Almost every day. And it's not the same."

Anything else he has to say is drowned out by my screams as the cab pulls up and Rayna pops out of the backseat, arms spread. I race to her, and we hug almost tight enough to feel it through our layers of coats and sweaters. By the time we pull apart, Sage has already paid the cabdriver and has Rayna's suitcase halfway to the door.

"Wow! Thanks, Sage."

"My pleasure," he says, holding the door open for us. Before she steps inside, Rayna gives him a huge hug and a peck on the cheek.

"It's really good to see you."

"Good to see you, too, Rayna."

I'm so happy watching them I could burst. I used to think it could never happen, that Rayna would always look at Sage and be heartbroken for Nico, but it's not like that at all. After everything that happened, Rayna said she knew Nico was at peace. It was still awkward for her at first. Even a month later, when she left for Paris, there was a tinge of weirdness between them—and us, to be honest—but pretty soon they were like old friends and we were back to normal. I've even come home from class, late for a planned Skype call, and found the two of them talking and laughing without me. It's pretty amazing. I have to give Rayna a lot of props for being so strong.

When we get in, I take Rayna's arm and give her the grand tour. We have the basement unit of the brownstone. Mom would have bought us something more—she offered a huge apartment in the Village—but Sage and I wanted to live a normal life. Our apartment isn't huge, and it's not superluxurious, but it's all we need, and we love it.

"You are *so* much better off here than in a dorm," she says. "Totally worth having your mom call in the favor."

"I hated to do it," I say, plopping down with her on the couch, "but I couldn't live with Sage in NYU freshman housing, and I'm sorry, but I didn't want to wait a year before we moved in together."

"Of course not! You waited long enough."

Sage brings in a tray with a cheese plate and three glasses of wine.

"Check you out, all domestic," Rayna says.

"Gets better," Sage says. "I specifically picked a Malbec from a French vineyard, in your honor."

"So you say," she says swirling the wine in her glass. "I'm dubious." Then she takes a sip. "Wow. Okay, yes. This is the real thing."

"Feels like you're back in Paris?" Sage asks.

"*Nothing* feels like Paris," Rayna says.

It was a huge surprise when she decided to take a year off before college and go to Europe. Rayna had never been that far from home on her own. Wanda freaked out, and even though I didn't admit it to Rayna, I was even a little skeptical. But she was incredible. She thought she'd spend the whole year just wandering, but soon after she landed in Paris she heard about an opening for an intern at the top French fashion magazine. I forget the name, but I know she loves it, she feels she's found herself, and we're all wondering if she's going to ever come back permanently.

"Pictures of Aaron," I say. "You promised."

"I didn't take any!"

"Rayna! You've been together for, like, two months! I'd think you'd be planning your wedding by now!"

She shrugs. "I don't know. He's nice. I really

like him. I just want to take it slow. But if we're talking about pictures, can we discuss how your apartment is basically an art gallery?"

I roll my eyes, and Sage laughs. Our stuff is hardly impressive enough to count as gallery material, but Sage draws all the time now, and his best charcoals are framed on the walls, along with some of my photography. There's not a lot, since most of what I shoot lately is for school. The photography major is excellent, but I have to slog through the intro courses first. I'm learning a lot, but it's not like I'm getting a lot of frame-worthy material.

Hours go by before she brings up the one topic we've avoided by Skype.

"He calls me sometimes, you know. I always feel weird. Like I'm betraying you guys if I take the call."

"You're not," I assure her.

"It's not like we talk often. He doesn't have a whole lot to say, really."

"I thought things were going well for him. He's teaching in California, right?"

"Yeah. Did I tell you that?"

"Mom did. He keeps her posted, and she tells me some things."

"Got it. So yeah, things are good and all. It's just whenever he talks to me, he only ends up telling me how much he wants you back in his life. *Both* of you," she adds, nodding to Sage.

Sage holds up his hands. "It's all Clea. I'm good with whatever she wants."

I shake my head. I miss Ben's friendship too. We shared so much. . . . In some ways, even after all this time living together, not even Sage knows me as well as he did. But he betrayed us too many times. And the last time . . .

I used to think about it a lot. I wondered if it was even his fault. Magda could have been clearer when she told me about the ceremony. She gave me only enough information that I'd have to turn to Ben for help. Did she know he'd find a way to sabotage it? Once he discovered it, did he ever have a chance of resisting, or was he doomed to fall right back into that pattern that had always haunted the three of us? Was that Magda's plan all along, or was she genuinely trying to help, and did Ben betray us all on his own?

For a long time, I tortured myself over it. I even thought about hiring someone to track down Magda in her new life and grill her about it. But in the end, I didn't want to dig up old ghosts. I needed to put all the ugliness behind me if I really wanted to make a fresh start with Sage.

That meant putting Ben behind me too. I don't hate him. I'm not even mad at him — I won't give him that kind of energy. I just can't have him in my life.

"Can't do it," I say. "I wish him well, though. I do."

Rayna nods and takes a sip of her wine, then starts to laugh. It's infectious, and soon Sage and I are laughing along with her, even though we have no idea why.

"What is it?" I ask.

"Clea, look at us! It was only a year ago we were getting ready for our big trip to Europe. If you'd told us then where we'd be right now . . . do you think we'd ever believe it?"

Nobody would believe everything we've been through, but I know what she means. A year ago I'd never even seen Sage, and Rayna wouldn't have dreamed of living on her own.

"Never in a million years," I say.

Rayna's laughter subsides, and something washes over her. "Do you ever wonder if it can last?"

"What do you mean?"

"Things are so good now. I'm happy, you and Sage are happy. . . . It's so night-and-day from where we were, but it feels perfect now, you know?"

"I do."

"So what if a year from *now* everything is completely different again?"

I think about it. I look at Sage, at our little apartment filled with his drawings and all my college assignments. I look at Rayna, glowing with inner confidence. And I smile.

"Things will change," I say. "But I'm not worried about it. You know why?"

"Why?"

"Because the most important things in life . . . they're eternal."

acknowledgments

HELLO AGAIN!

Wow, I cannot believe book three is finally finished! What a journey this has been. A huge thank-you to all of my lovely fans who have been dedicated to this trilogy and to me from the beginning. It has been incredible to travel around the world and see my books translated into many different languages — having the opportunity to meet many of you face-to-face and see your enthusiasm is something I will never forget! You are the ones who inspire me every day to try new things, and this book is the perfect example. Thank you for your passion.

I feel very lucky to have worked with the amazingly talented and spirited Elise Allen, who helped create these books with me and took our characters on a wild ride. I love that we had absolute honesty and respect for each other through this process. You are genius and I love you!

Fonda and Rob, thank you for believing in me and for guiding me through this process. Your expertise was greatly appreciated, and your creative opinions always made for positive changes.

To my wonderful team at Simon & Schuster who really made this all happen, you guys have been great partners and I appreciate all of the hard work from you: Zareen Jaffery, Julia Maguire, Carolyn Reidy, Jon Anderson, Justin Chanda, Anne Zafian, Paul Crichton, Nicole Russo, Lucille Rettino, Jenica Nasworthy, and Lizzy Bromley.

XXO
HD